Sleight of Hand

by

Shawna Delacorte

Sleight of Hand

Cover Art by *Diana Carlile.*

The Wild Rose Press, Inc.
PO Box 708
Adams Basin, NY 14410-0708
Visit us at www.thewildrosepress.com

Publishing History
First Edition, 2025
Trade Paperback ISBN 978-1-5092-6050-8
Digital ISBN 978-1-5092-6049-2

Published in the United States of America

Chapter One

"It's two o'clock in the morning," Huntington Wolfe III growled into the phone. "This better be important."

"Hunt, it's Leo Jordan. Sorry about waking you. I've got an assignment that's perfect for you, in addition to being literally in your backyard."

"What is it?"

"Jewelry. Counting the most recent theft, Excellence Insurance's portion over five years exceeds twenty million U.S. dollars in insured value and that doesn't take into consideration what other insurance companies have lost. Each theft has occurred following some sort of society event or charity fund raiser. It's a circle of the upper crust our staff of investigators can't seem to get close to even in an undercover capacity. You live and function among the wealthy. You're personal friends with them. I thought you might have easier access, could get inside without arousing suspicion. The police haven't been forthcoming with information. I've had to go through other sources to be kept up to date."

Hunt rubbed sleep from his eyes. "My usual forty percent of the insured value for anything I recover, plus a bonus if I provide the proof needed to successfully prosecute those responsible?"

"That's our deal. I'll send you all the information I have, along with a contract for your services."

"There's a charity benefit in two days that exactly fits the type of events the thief has been targeting over the last five years. I received an invitation, but I find those functions boring and usually decline. I sent a donation along with my regrets for being unable to attend. Now, it looks like I need to revise my schedule."

They talked a couple of minutes longer, then Hunt terminated the phone conversation. He glanced at the clock. The eight-hour time difference between London and Seattle sometimes made for inconvenient business hours. The possibility of getting back to sleep had slipped away, and he was now wide awake.

He opened the French doors that led from his second-floor bedroom suite to the balcony overlooking his back yard, his private dock, and out to Lake Washington. Moonlight glinted off the water. A slight chill hit his bare chest, the floor tile cold on his bare feet. He breathed in the clean night air. Whether daylight or a moonlit night, he never tired of the view.

Hunt's body stiffened. His senses jumped on full alert. A sudden movement in the shadows grabbed his attention. A figure darted across the lawn. He immediately flew into action, reacting instinctively to the intrusion without regard for the danger. He climbed over the balcony railing and dropped twelve feet to the lawn. Landing with a thud, he executed an expert tuck-and-roll, then jumped to his feet.

He fought to maintain his balance as his bare feet slipped on the wet grass. Finally regaining his footing, he dashed in the direction the intruder had gone. He rounded the corner of his house. His heart pounded as he caught sight of his quarry headed toward the high stone wall bordering the front and sides of his property with the back defined by the lake. Digging his feet into the lawn, he raced full speed toward the culprit.

"Damn!" His cry broke the stillness of the night. His breath caught in his throat as a sharp pain shot up his leg when his foot came down hard on one of the sprinkler heads of the lawn watering system. Hopping on the other foot, he winced in pain as he tried to maintain his balance. In spite of his efforts, he ended up on his ass in a muddy flower bed. He watched helplessly as the intruder scaled the wall using a rope that must have been set in place as a means of making a speedy escape. The rope quickly disappeared over the wall, the culprit taking it with him.

The sound of tires squealing on the pavement reached his ears as a vehicle sped away. By the time he limped down the long driveway, opened the gates, and emerged onto the street, whoever had invaded his property had totally disappeared into the night without any hint to which direction the vehicle had gone.

****

Hunt walked out onto the elaborately decorated terrace of Carl and Eleanor Swanson's Mercer Island mansion. His practiced eye darted from ring to necklace to earrings adorning the women at the affair as he made a quick appraisal of the jewelry's worth, any one of the items a tempting target on its own. A ripple of excitement moved through him, bringing back the thrill of days gone by. He sucked in a steadying breath to calm the familiar reaction to a tempting situation as it clawed its way out of the depth of the emotional vault where he had locked it away. He had long ago purged the desire to act on the impulse.

He wandered over to where the Swansons were

greeting their guests. "Carl...Eleanor, good to see you." He gave Eleanor a kiss on the cheek, then the two men shook hands.

He eyed the stunning emerald hanging around Eleanor's neck, definitely the most spectacular piece of jewelry on display. The flawless twenty-five carat emerald pendant surrounded by diamonds in a platinum setting had been in Carl's family for generations.

"That's certainly an impressive rock, Eleanor. Aren't you a little nervous about having it out of the bank vault, considering the thefts over the last five years...especially since they now seem to have started up again after a brief pause?"

"Maybe that depends on you, Hunt?" Her voice and smile teased, but her eyes conveyed a hint of truth hidden in her words.

He allowed a good-natured laugh in spite of her implied accusation. "Now really, Eleanor. You don't still believe those old tales and rumors about me, do you? Those were started over ten years ago. I have more money than I can count. Why would I want to jeopardize my lifestyle and risk prison by stealing jewelry that I don't want and certainly don't need?"

"I don't know..." She extended a knowing smile. "Perhaps for the challenge?" She tilted her head and raised a questioning eyebrow. "Or maybe the thrill?"

A tingle of anticipation reverberated inside him, the one associated with just that type of challenge and the subsequent thrill. An amused chuckle accompanied his words, one he hoped didn't sound as forced as it felt. "I get all the thrills I need piloting my own jet, scuba diving the Great Barrier Reef, and skiing the Alps. Besides, I wasn't even in the country when some of the thefts occurred…including the last one."

Hunt's airtight alibi of being out of the country for some of the dates had aggravated Lt. Montrose when he had once again hauled Hunt into police headquarters and aggressively interrogated him about the latest outbreak of jewelry thefts based on nothing more than Montrose's desire for him to be guilty. And Hunt purposely pushed the lieutenant's exasperation by politely answering the questions without benefit of his attorney until he had reached the limit of his patience and abruptly ended the interrogation. He'd walked out, leaving his nemesis fuming but unable to do anything about it.

He dismissed the thoughts as he casually glanced around the Swanson's terrace observing the socially elite in attendance. Then his gaze landed on a man in his early sixties. Hunt's jaw tightened and his muscles tensed. "Carl…Eleanor…please excuse me. I see someone headed this way that I'd like to avoid." He quickly lost himself in the crowd.

"Champagne, sir?"

The throaty, feminine voice instantly grabbed his attention. His gaze fell on the tall, leggy blonde holding the tray of glasses. "Thank you—" He leaned forward and stared at her chest, making an obvious point of reading her name tag. "—Gwen." He flashed his patently sexy smile as he took one of the glasses while making a quick yet thorough appraisal of her physical attributes.

Charlie Gorman sure knows how to pick the women who work for his catering company.

She appeared to be in her late twenties, maybe thirty-years-old. An aura of cool efficiency accompanied her blue-eyed gaze, one that left him with the strange sensation of someone delving into his psyche in an attempt to ferret out his secrets. An uneasy reaction stirred inside him, one he couldn't quite identify beyond the fact that it put his senses on full alert.

She wore the same work attire as all the attractive women who worked at Prestige Caterers—black satin shorts and vest, white long-sleeved shirt with French cuffs, black bowtie, and black fishnet stockings. He watched as she circulated among the guests while handling her duties. Her smile, the way she moved, clothes that hugged her enticing curves without being overtly suggestive.

"Hunt...I haven't seen you for a while." A hand clamped down on his shoulder, drawing his attention away from the decidedly erotic fantasy rapidly taking shape in his mind. He stifled the groan that formed the moment he recognized the voice. His attempt to lose himself in the crowd obviously hadn't succeeded. The impeccably dressed man greeted him with a warm smile. "I was out of town on business and missed the last gala. How have you been?"

Hunt shook his hand and forced a casual outer attitude and friendly smile as the annoyance spread through his body. "You know me, I'm wherever there's a party. I just returned from a couple of weeks in Tahiti, only been home a few days."

The man chuckled. "I must admit I'm a little envious of your lifestyle. Most of my travels these days are business related. And let me tell you..." He glanced around as if to make sure no one could hear him then lowered his voice as an extra precaution. "The little woman has really been on my case about it lately. She thinks I should be sending someone else on these trips. She just doesn't understand the reality of the situation.

Women simply don't have the capacity to deal with the complexities of big business."

Hunt suppressed the jolt of disgust that sliced through him. *The little woman? I'll bet you don't call her that when she can hear you. And you think women aren't capable of understanding big business? That's both stupid and ignorant.* As far as Hunt was concerned, the man was a Neanderthal recently chipped out of a glacier where he had been frozen for centuries with no concept of today's reality.

It was the same kind of thing his father used to say, the identical condescending comment and patronizing attitude his mother resented. Hunt was an only child who came from a rich and powerful family with generations of old-line money on both his father's and mother's side, yet the household where he grew up had been totally dysfunctional. Having read a couple of psychology books about it, he had come to the conclusion that becoming a successful jewel thief and cat burglar was his means of rebelling against what he considered the chaos that surrounded his childhood and teen years, a situation where he had no control.

He glanced toward Gwen, catching sight of her as she disappeared inside the house carrying a tray of empty glasses. He quickly yet reluctantly turned his attention to his conversation, making an attempt to break it off without being rude. "Well, sending someone else on those business trips is something to consider, maybe your executive vice president. Take him with you on the next trip. You can introduce him to the people he needs to know." He held up his empty champagne glass and flashed an apologetic smile. "I think I need a refill. Please excuse me."

The moment he reached the doorway from the terrace into the house, Hunt came to an abrupt halt. He was seldom caught by surprise, but the scene that greeted him was the last thing he expected to see. Ducking around a corner out of sight, he watched as Gwen deftly picked the pocket of one of the guests, her actions so subtle and quick that most people wouldn't have realized what she had done even if they had seen it. She slipped the wallet inside her vest and continued on toward the kitchen.

A hint of a smile tugged the corners of his mouth as Hunt embraced a moment of appreciation for her skill— a highly professional job with her mark not having a clue. Anyone who could lift a wallet that proficiently wouldn't have any trouble making off with a piece of expensive jewelry. Of course, there would still be the problem of the security system and breaking into a safe.

Hunt adopted a casual manner as he walked toward the kitchen. He spotted her inside the pantry going through the contents of the wallet, her expression showing her displeasure at what she found. Or perhaps the more accurate conclusion would be her displeasure at what she didn't find. She put the wallet inside her vest and grabbed a tray of filled champagne glasses.

"Ah...Gwen." Hunt flashed a dazzling smile as he stepped in front of her, blocking her way as she emerged from the kitchen. "Just the person I was looking for."

He took a full glass from the tray and replaced it with his empty one. She nervously gave a quick glance toward the owner of the wallet, something most people wouldn't have noticed. It was the only indication of anything being amiss. Everything else about her demeanor projected a cool, in control composure, her radiant smile in place.

That she was a beautiful and incredibly desirable woman went without saying. But there was more. She fascinated him, every bit as much as the game she seemed to be playing. He definitely needed to know more about Gwen as someone possibly connected to the case.

Hunt circulated among the party guests, easily engaging in idle conversation with the wealthy and socially prominent—families that had been associated with his own through generations of old established society, people he had known all his life. As he made his way comfortably through the privileged, wealthy, and powerful, he kept a vigilant eye on Gwen.

Then his outwardly casual manner took another hit when her next action totally threw him for a loop. He stood riveted to the spot, mesmerized, and watched as she approached her mark.

She held out the wallet toward him. "Excuse me, sir. I believe you dropped this."

The startled man immediately reached for his pocket. A shocked expression raced across his face when he discovered his wallet missing. He took it from her hand and quickly checked his credit cards and money. Apparently satisfied that nothing was missing, he handed her a hundred-dollar bill. "Thank you, young lady. I hadn't even missed it. Here's a little something for your trouble and your honesty."

She shook her head and extended a friendly smile. "I can't accept that, sir. Thank you, anyway." She continued circulating with the tray of champagne glasses.

Hunt watched her as he ran the facts through his

mind, bits of information that initially seemed to have nothing in common.

A stranger scaled the wall of my estate in the middle of the night, yet didn't enter my home. An employee of the catering company lifted a wallet from a guest then returned it intact a few minutes later. Two entirely unrelated incidents that occurred within a couple of days of each other. Both happened right after I agreed to handle the jewel theft investigation for Leo Jordan, the CEO of Excellence Insurance half a world away in London, England. A coincidence?

Not likely.

Huntington Wolfe III did not believe in strange, inexplicable coincidences. There had to be some kind of connection between the two occurrences even though they seemed miles apart.

Before he had time to give her odd behavior any further consideration, he was pulled into a conversation about membership rules at the Yacht Club. He covered his boredom and feigned an interest in the discussion. But his attention never strayed far from Gwen. His curiosity about what he had seen continued to simmer, threatening to force all other thoughts from his mind— all except how desirable he found Gwen, those lustful thoughts he hadn't been able to completely set aside.

He stayed behind after most of the guests had departed, chatting amiably with Carl Swanson while keeping an eye on Gwen. As soon as he saw her head for the door to leave, he extended his goodbye to the Swansons and hurried to catch up to her.

He noted her car license number, but she was out of sight before he could get to his car. He emitted a little sigh of resignation mixed with disappointment.

Probably just as well. My red Porsche isn't exactly an inconspicuous car for tailing someone, and I don't want to put her on alert.

He drove home to Medina, an exclusive upscale town in the greater Seattle area just north of Bellevue, located on the east shore of Lake Washington. He stifled a yawn as he paused while the gates to his estate swung open.

His thoughts returned to his phone conversation with Leo Jordan. Leo was one of only three people who knew the truth about those five years of his life when he was the world's most successful cat burglar and jewel thief. He had reconciled that tumultuous five-year period with the knowledge that it was primarily an attempt to rebel against society.

Then there was also the fact that he had grown bored of always staying two steps ahead of Lt. Montrose. And now, Hunt worked as a private investigator, tracking down jewel thieves for Leo Jordan.

He chuckled softly. Who better to catch a thief than a former thief?

****

The next morning, Hunt sat at his desk in his home office as he gazed out the window. The morning sun sparkled off the water of Lake Washington. The serene view always brought a sense of calm and helped him work his way through annoying problems. His small, sixteen-foot sailboat bobbed in the water where it was tied to his private dock. Even though his dock could accommodate a much larger boat, he usually kept his seventy-five-foot cabin cruiser at the Yacht Club.

He sipped his coffee and continued to stare out at the water. A viable plan of action began to form in his mind.

After checking the time, he grabbed the phone and hit the speed dial button for Records at the Seattle Police Department. A moment later the familiar voice of his cousin came on the line.

"Records, Sgt. Cosgrove."

"Rita, I've got an out of state license plate for you to run. I want the name and address of the car's registered owner."

"Not even a *good morning* from you?" Her irritation came across loud and clear. "Just another of your *I want* favors?"

"Come on, Rita. I'm in a hurry. Could we dispense with the usual lecture this time?"

"You're always in a hurry when you want a favor from me. I told you last time I wasn't going to do any more of these for you."

"Yeah, I know." He couldn't stop the spontaneous laugh. "But you're always telling me that. It's pretty much lost its effectiveness."

"All right, give me the number." Exasperation surrounded her words. "I can't do it right now. I'll call you back in a little bit, probably a couple of hours."

Hunt filled the time waiting for Rita's call by once again going over the information Leo Jordan had sent him. Twelve jewel thefts in the last five years and not a clue as to who or how. Even though two had happened on the same night, the police believed they were all the work of the same person. Then there was that business with Quentin Brentano being the chief suspect. A high-speed chase with the police, resulting in his car bursting into flames when it hit the rocks below the cliff.

A snort of disdain matched his thoughts. *Cars occasionally might explode when they go over cliffs and hit the rocks below but not usually. That's a special effects movie stunt. Something to look good on the screen and add excitement to the car chase. Not a normal part of real life.*

He furrowed his brow as he shook his head. Something was wrong, very wrong, but he couldn't put his finger on it.

Quentin's body has not been found. The official theory says whatever remained after the explosion and subsequent fire had washed out to sea and ended up as fish food. Although there was a brief mention in an early news story about a phone found lodged between two rocks, the claim of not finding anything at the crash site doesn't ring true. Not finding anything that would positively identify the body—maybe. But to find nothing at all? Not even a trace of his body? No bone fragments? Not a scrap of fabric from his clothes? Absolutely no trace evidence of any kind? I'm not buying it!

"—another spectacular jewelry caper." The television news story broke into his thoughts. The Swanson Emerald had turned up missing that morning. As with most of the robbery victims, the Swansons normally kept their high value jewelry in a safe deposit box at the bank. On special occasions, the necklace was taken from the bank to be worn then returned to the bank vault the next business day. In the interim, it was kept in a high tech safe at their house.

He stared at the phone on his desk. A ripple of annoyance attached itself to his impatience. He hated being at someone else's mercy, of having to wait while someone else worked his needs into their schedule. He knew Rita would get him what he wanted.

In spite of her ongoing protests, she always came

through for him. They were first cousins and had grown up together. She was the only relative he cared about, the only one he was close to in a sea of dysfunctional family members scattered around the world.

His mother had died four years ago and his father two years later, leaving him as head of the family empire, the sole beneficiary of both parents. In spite of his current perceived jet-setting playboy lifestyle, he kept a close watch on the day-to-day business of the numerous Wolfe financial interests. He made no attempt to micromanage and didn't believe in hiring a bunch of yes men who would be telling him what they thought he wanted to hear. He surrounded himself with intelligent, capable people and gave them the room to do their jobs without his constant interference.

Rita was the only family member he trusted, at least to a point. He had told her he was a private investigator, something to do that he enjoyed with money not being a consideration. He accepted only the cases that truly interested him. He never mentioned the on-going relationship with Leo Jordan and Excellence Insurance. As far as he knew, she thought of the P.I. stints as his current *hobby*.

He paced up and down his office until the pent-up tension forced him into action. He grabbed the phone and placed a call to Leo Jordan in London. "Did you hear about the most recent robbery? The Swanson's emerald disappeared last night following a charity benefit at their house. Do you carry the policy on the Swanson's jewelry?"

"No. At this point, I'm pleased to say that one isn't ours. Her emerald is somebody else's headache. Do you think it's part of this string of jewel thefts?"

"The only way it could *not* be connected is for the Swansons to have staged the theft themselves to swindle the insurance company." A hint of sarcasm accompanied Hunt's words. "I know for a fact that their financial situation is solid. They don't need to file a false insurance claim in order to get their hands on some ready cash. I personally saw the emerald last night when Eleanor wore it. As an expert on gemstones, I assure you it was the genuine article, not a copy."

Hunt terminated his conversation with Leo then placed a call to Prestige Caterers. Charlie Gorman's catering business was aptly named. It was the best around, due in large part to the expertise of his chef, Stu Allen. Prestige Caterers was the choice of the wealthy and socially elite. They did almost all the large parties, society functions, and charity events held in private residences. Clients had been known to change the date of their events to accommodate Charlie's schedule. Hunt had used Prestige Caterers on several occasions for his entertainment needs.

"Charlie? It's Hunt Wolfe." He kept his conversation breezy, projecting the playboy-at-large image Charlie expected. He lowered his voice to a conspiratorial level. "You had a sexy little number working for you at the Swanson's party last night. Her name is Gwen. About five feet seven inches, blonde hair, big blue eyes, the most terrific legs I've seen in a long time, and—" He paused for dramatic effect to make sure he had Charlie's full attention. "—a body that could make a grown man tremble in anticipation."

"Yeah, I know *exactly* what you mean." Charlie's lecherous tone said more than his words. "She's a tasty looking treat."

"I know you don't normally do this, but could you give me her last name and phone number? I tried to hit on her but failed miserably. You'll be pleased to know she was all business and stuck to doing her job, although I have to admit it was a bit of a blow to my ego." Hunt allowed a lascivious chuckle to drive his point home. "And definitely *her* loss."

"Her name's Gwen York. She's only been with the company about six weeks. Claimed she just moved to town from Chicago, but her car has California license plates. I normally wouldn't give out personal information, but for you..." A knowing laugh exactly conveyed the thoughts going through his mind. "Hold on while I find her phone number."

He heard Charlie clicking on the keyboard at his computer. Next came a pause followed by the sound of papers being shuffled.

"Hunt? You still there?"

"Yep, standing by."

"This is weird. I don't seem to have a phone number for her. All I have is a pager number. My scheduling coordinator has a note here indicating that's the only means of contact. Do you want that number?"

"A pager?" A spontaneous laugh escaped his throat. "That's certainly antiquated. I didn't know pagers were still available what with smart phones being able to do just about everything except shovel the snow off the driveway. But I guess they can send instructions to the robot that actually does the shoveling. Sure, give it to me."

Hunt wrote down the information then quickly terminated the conversation. He could take only so much of the *good ol' boy, wink-wink, nudge-nudge* talk with

Charlie. And it didn't take long for him to reach that limit.

He poured another cup of coffee then stepped out onto the terrace, his mind sifting through the little bit of information he had garnered. The ringing of his phone intruded into his thoughts.

"What do you have for me, Rita?" He started to jot down the information then stopped in stunned silence. This was the second time in less than twenty-four hours he had been caught by surprise—watching Gwen's pickpocket trick last night and now the information Rita had supplied. He found his voice, the words a mere whisper. "I'll be damned."

He wrote down the rest of the information then promised Rita they would get together sometime soon for dinner. Leaning back in his chair, he stared at the paper in his hand. He let out a long, low whistle.

"I sure wasn't expecting this." His words escaped into the open even though there wasn't anyone around to hear them. "I can scratch item number one off my to-do list. I found Gwen York. And apparently, I can also cross item number two off that list. According to the California Department of Motor Vehicles, the car Gwen York drove when leaving the Swanson's party is registered to Aurora Brentano, Quentin Brentano's daughter who lives in San Francisco."

Chapter Two

"So...what's new?" Johnny O'Brian wandered into Hunt's office and eased his six-four frame into the chair. The forty-two-year-old could easily have passed as a football linebacker still in his prime. However, the scar across his cheek and previously broken nose—the result of an automobile accident several years ago—made him look more like a mob enforcer.

Hunt looked up at the sound of the voice. "Hi, Johnny. When did you get back?"

"About two o'clock this morning."

"How's your father?"

"Doing much better—out of the hospital and resting at home. He sends his regards." Johnny poured himself a cup of coffee. "Any follow up on whoever tried to break in here while I was gone?"

"Nothing new on that."

"Bring me up to date on the jewelry thefts. What's happened since your last text from yesterday morning?"

"I ran into a weird situation at the Swanson's party last night, and I don't know what it means. Then this morning I heard on the news that the Swanson Emerald was stolen last night before Eleanor could get it back to the bank. I just talked to Leo Jordan. He said they don't have the policy on it. But this is obviously part of the same string of thefts."

"Since you were at that party, are we going to

include it as part of our investigation for Leo?"

Johnny lived in the two-bedroom guest house on the grounds of Hunt's estate. He had worked as Hunt's right-hand man from the first day Hunt formed Mask Incorporated as a holding company to hide his direct involvement with Leo Jordan and Excellence Insurance. Prior to that, Johnny and Hunt had a different relationship. Johnny had been the best fence in the business and Hunt a superb cat burglar—a perfect match and a lucrative arrangement. Johnny was another of the three people who knew about Hunt's cat burglar background.

At the age of twenty-eight, Hunt came to grips with his unresolved problems of being the only heir to the two fortunes of a totally dysfunctional family. He called it quits as a jewel thief before he pressed his luck too far and ended up in prison. That was six years ago. At that time, Johnny came to work for him in a different capacity, helping with the investigations for Excellence Insurance and any other cases Hunt chose to accept.

Even though Hunt had excellent computer skills, Johnny's were exceptional. He had the ability to be a world-class hacker of the most sophisticated security software. He loved all kinds of electronic gadgets. Like Hunt, he was also highly intelligent and resourceful. Together, they made a formidable team.

"Yes, we'll include it as part of our investigation. It's obviously part of this string of thefts. I'd like to see the Swansons get their emerald back. It's been in Carl's family for several generations. It means a lot more to them than just the monetary worth. It has a high sentimental value. He once showed me a picture of his mother wearing it at a charity benefit."

"Where are you with the investigation? Where do you want me to begin?"

"I think we'll start with Quentin Brentano."

"But isn't he dead?" Johnny extended a questioning look. "Died in that car crash while being chased by the cops—specifically Montrose and his sidekick?"

"So it appears, but I wonder…" Hunt furrowed his brow in concentration.

As he did with everything that struck him as a potential case, he had made a file on the jewel thefts. When the police named Quentin Brentano as their major person of interest in the thefts, Hunt made a file on him, too. He didn't know anything about Quentin's daughter other than the newspaper obituary listing her as his next of kin living in San Francisco. He turned on his computer, pulled up the files on the thefts and Quentin, then retrieved the manila folder containing some newspaper clippings that hadn't been available online, ones he had not yet scanned into his computer.

He forwarded a copy of the computer files to Johnny's computer and handed him the envelope of clippings. "Would you mind adding these to the computer files?"

Johnny took the folder. "Sure, no problem."

"If Quentin is dead, it certainly came at an extremely convenient time. Add to that the woman working for Prestige Caterers at last night's soirée, wearing a name tag that said Gwen but drove away in a car registered to Aurora Brentano, and…"

"You think this guy is still alive? It seems to me if he faked his own death to get the cops off his back, it would be stupid for him to continue ripping off jewelry—at least in the same part of the country where he had been plying his trade. If it was me and I'd just faked my death, I'd be out of town so fast you wouldn't even see my dust. I sure wouldn't stick around so I could pull more jobs in the same place following the same pattern."

"Yeah…me, too. Just one of several inconsistencies that don't make any sense."

"So, any preference about where you want me to start, or can I handle it at my discretion?"

"First on the list is Aurora Brentano. The car registration shows a San Francisco address. Find out when she left San Francisco, whether she was anywhere else between leaving there and ending up here, or if she came straight to Seattle. I need to know where she's staying. Scope out her father's house in Bellevue. That's the most logical place for her to be."

"Unless she's in hiding and staying off the grid."

"If that's the case, then it seems to me she wouldn't be driving her own car with the California license plates. I'm guessing she's being cautious but doesn't think anyone's actually looking for her."

Johnny nodded. "If her father's house doesn't pan out, I'll check the utilities to see if there's anything in her name in the greater Seattle area and surrounding towns. If that doesn't turn something, I'll hit the motels that rent suites on a monthly basis."

"Check both names…Aurora Brentano and Gwen York. All I have for Gwen is a pager number that Charlie Gorman gave me, no phone number. Apparently, not even a disposable cell phone. At least not one that Charlie knows about. Locate an existing phone number, and see if you can track her location through the GPS chip and cell towers from her phone calls. If that doesn't work, maybe you can find a local address through Gwen's pager." Hunt texted the pager number to Johnny.

After Johnny left, Hunt refilled his coffee mug and stepped out on the terrace again. He stared at the water. Closing his eyes, he sucked in a deep breath, held it for a few seconds, then slowly exhaled. No matter where in the world he traveled, to what exotic location, it always soothed his soul to return home. He took another deep breath, then once again turned his thoughts to the business at hand.

There's a lot more going on with this case than just the theft of some high-dollar jewelry. But what? Could the police theory be right? Quentin Brentano did it and now his partner is continuing with the thefts? A partner who just happens to also be his daughter?

The image of delectable Aurora played across the screen of his mind. His breathing quickened. He might have been doing a number on Charlie Gorman in order to get the information he wanted, but he couldn't deny the way she made his pulse race or the serious impact this woman had on his libido.

No question about it, she represented a definite obstacle to his investigation.

****

Aurora Brentano turned on her laptop computer and pulled up the file on the string of jewelry thefts, as she had done each morning since her arrival in Seattle four days after her father's death. Once again, she perused her list of suspects. And topping that list? Her number one suspect—Huntington Wolfe III. She read the personal information she had gathered on him for what seemed like the hundredth time, information she had long ago memorized. Thirty-four years old, never married, six feet one inch tall, dark hair and green eyes, educated at the best schools, fluent in five languages and a passable command of two more, the only child and sole heir to the Wolfe family fortune as well as another fortune on his mother's side, international playboy with no visible means of support other than living off the extensive family wealth.

A perfect example of a member of the idle rich who wouldn't know how to do an honest day's work if his life depended on it with an emphasis on *honest*. Rumor had it he was a notorious cat burglar who had committed a string of jewel thefts—all across Europe as well as domestic—before retiring with an unblemished record of no arrests, even though he had been questioned several times. And as with all the other thefts in this recent string, he was one of only a handful of people who had been at several of the events where jewelry had been stolen.

She allowed a slight frown, accompanied by a brief moment of doubt. *He wasn't present at all of the events, just some of them. He was also probably at several events where nothing was stolen.*

A quick surge of disgust darted through her consciousness before she could stop it. She shook her head in an attempt to clear the totally inappropriate thoughts. She couldn't declare someone guilty based on nothing more than her personal prejudices concerning his lifestyle. Being a member of the idle rich who always had everything he wanted—someone with no direction, ambition, or purpose—didn't mean he had anything to do with the thefts.

He was the type of person she resented for his lack of concern for those who didn't come from his privileged background, those who didn't have everything handed to them, those who struggled with day-to-day life.

She leaned back in her chair, closed her eyes, and visualized his face from the party. Regardless of her disdain of his lifestyle, she had to admit the newspaper photos did not do him justice. They didn't reveal the dimples when he flashed that sexy smile, nor did they show the devilish sparkle in his green eyes. And then there was the mesmerizing quality of his smooth voice, something she could not have gotten from the newspaper articles.

She jerked to attention. Her eyes snapped open as she sat up straight. What was there about this disconcerting man that continued to tempt her, beckoning her toward him?

Her research information showed he owned a seventy-five-foot power yacht, a private jet, which he piloted himself, a thirty-million-dollar estate in Medina that backed up on Lake Washington listed as his primary residence, and vacation houses in Switzerland and on the French Riviera.

Switzerland means the possibility of a numbered bank account with secret deposits. Yet more trappings of the wealthy and privileged. That bit of information had moved him from among her many suspects to the top of her list.

A moment of sorrow about her father's death tried to take hold, but anger quickly replaced it. She clenched her jaw into a hard line of determination and reinforced her resolve. Not for one moment did she believe her father had committed the crimes. She intended to prove his innocence and clear his name, no matter how long it took or whose toes she stepped on.

The police had been no help at all. Numerous phone conversations with them from San Francisco had resulted in total frustration. Nothing could be accomplished by trying to contact them after she arrived in Seattle to arrange a face-to-face meeting. Only one option presented itself. In order to achieve her goal, she needed to identify the guilty party on her own.

On-going tension churned inside her, and a new wave of anger surged through her body reinforcing her determination. During her calls with the obnoxious Lt. Montrose, he had made it clear he held her father responsible for the stolen jewelry and refused to give it further discussion. Her primary objective was to clear her father's name, but she couldn't deny being compelled to also bring down Montrose's smug arrogance and make him publicly eat his words about her father.

She returned her thoughts to her current plan of action. *Step one is to figure out how to make personal contact with Huntington Wolfe III without making him suspicious. Establishing some sort of personal connection with him will make my investigation easier.*

She had even scaled the wall surrounding his estate hoping to get some kind of information she could use. A cold shudder assaulted her senses as she recalled the moment she saw a man emerge from the house and stand on a second-floor balcony. She had bolted toward the wall surrounding the grounds with only one thought in mind—make it over the wall and to her car before someone saw her and called the police. Or worse yet, before someone took a shot at her. Ending up in jail or the hospital, neither had been on her agenda.

Reality had surprised her when her primary suspect

suddenly showed up at the Swanson's party. Doubt pushed at her followed by a rush of uncertainty.

It's too late now, but I should probably have been more receptive to his obvious flirting rather than being all business. Then another thought hit her with a sudden flash of alarm. *Had he seen me lift the wallet? No, he couldn't have. If he had seen me, wouldn't he have exposed my actions? Said something to someone? Or, much more likely*—another surge of disgust invaded her thoughts—*he would have demanded that I share the contents with him.*

She once again tightened her jaw. No one would ever convince her of her father's guilt. Lt. Montrose had literally hounded her father to his grave. A wave of despair washed over her, but she quickly wiped away the tears welling in her eyes.

Correction—hounded him to his death. They never recovered his body. He doesn't have a grave. No place where I can go and be close to him.

She would find the person responsible for the thefts and make Montrose look like the despicable fool she knew him to be, no matter how long it took.

Hunger pangs rumbled through her stomach, drawing her attention to the here and now. She glanced at the clock, almost noon. She walked the few blocks to the waterfront café, choosing a table outside on the deck. After giving the waiter her lunch order, she leaned back in the chair and sipped her wine as she watched the boats.

"Well…this is a pleasant surprise. Gwen, isn't it?" The smooth, masculine voice broke into her reverie.

She looked up to find Huntington Wolfe III standing next to her table. A quick jolt of apprehension hit her, creating a sudden rush of trepidation.

Hunt had a report from Johnny in less than an hour, confirming Aurora had been staying at her father's house. He found her choice of residence a bit confusing. She went to all the trouble to use a pager and a phony name to hide her identity yet drove her own car and stayed in her father's house. If she had been trying to conceal her identity, it had turned out to be nothing more than a half-hearted effort.

Between the two of them, Hunt and Johnny kept her under constant surveillance. This was the first time she had left the house since he had discovered her identity. Confusion danced across her features followed by a hint of wariness. The warning signal rang loud and clear in his mind, telling him to be careful in how he proceeded.

He extended a friendly smile. "You were working for Charlie Gorman at the Swanson's party a couple of nights ago. I was there, too…remember?"

"Oh…yes." She returned his smile. "You were the guy who kept hitting on me while I was trying to do my job."

"Guilty as charged." He indicated the empty chair at her table. Cocking his head, he extended a quizzical look. "You're not working now. Are you expecting someone?"

"No. I was just taking advantage of this nice sunny day. How about you? What brings you here?"

"I was in this area taking care of a business matter and stopped here to grab something to eat. May I join you? I'd be honored if you'd allow me to buy you lunch." He winked at her as a wry grin tugged at the corners of his mouth. "Maybe I can redeem myself for having made such a bad first impression at the Swanson's party."

"Maybe you can." She smiled as she gestured toward the chair. "Actually, I've already given my lunch order."

Hunt seated himself, motioned for the waiter, and placed his order. Then he settled back in the chair and perused the woman seated across from him. In the light of day, she was even more stunning than she had been at the party—the creamy texture of her flawless skin, her sparkling blue eyes, her blonde hair glistening in the sunlight. His breathing increased slightly as a heated surge of pure lust raced through his body.

Her brow wrinkled into a frown. "Why are you staring at me like that?"

The wariness in her eyes caught his attention, warning him to rein in his libidinous thoughts.

"You're a beautiful woman. I was merely appreciating the view."

"Perhaps if I knew who you were I could put that comment into a proper context."

"Huntington Wolfe III...at your service."

"What do people call you?"

"Well...I guess that depends on whether they're my friends or not. My friends call me Hunt. The others address me as Mr. Wolfe."

She gave him a questioning look as if turning something over in her mind. "And what should I call you?"

"I'd like to think we're going to be friends, so call me Hunt. And you're Gwen...Gwen who?"

"Gwen York. I just moved here from Chicago."

The waiter brought both food orders along with the glass of wine Hunt had ordered. He raised his glass toward her in the form of a toast. She held her glass up to his.

"It's nice to officially meet you, Gwen. Here's to the

start of a fun friendship."

They clinked glasses, and each took a sip of wine to seal the toast, then they turned their attention to eating lunch. The pressure to maintain polite, superficial conversation didn't exist when mouths were full of food.

As much as Aurora had wanted to devise some means of making contact with Hunt again, she had not been prepared for him to materialize from out of nowhere, to literally appear in front of her. And the way he kept looking at her… It felt quite different from *appreciating the view* as he had phrased it. He seemed to be seriously studying her as if trying to read her thoughts. But why?

She shoved her suspicions aside. He was obviously living up to his playboy reputation, hitting on her in hopes of getting her into bed.

A moment of irritation shoved the inappropriate thoughts aside. She had a serious agenda and needed to stick with it. She couldn't allow a desirable physical temptation to distract her from that goal.

"So, tell me, Hunt—" She leveled an appraising look at him as she took a steadying breath. "—what are you really doing here? And I mean something other than *being in the area.* Do you live here in Bellevue? It's a nice neighborhood, but it seems to me that someone of your standing would live in a much more affluent area."

She scrunched up the side of her mouth as an errant thought hit her. She wanted to see his reaction to her mentioning the town where he lived. "Of course, just across the north city limits of Bellevue is Medina and beyond that is Hunt's Point, both extremely opulent areas." She emitted a chuckle that she hoped sounded spontaneous as if she had just thought of something.

"Perhaps it would be more appropriate for someone named Hunt to live in Hunt's Point."

He shot a curious look back at her. "Someone of *my standing*? Didn't you tell me you had just moved here from Chicago? Are you saying I've been the subject of idle gossip in Chicago?" A teasing grin tugged at the corners of his mouth. "I've been to Chicago several times, but I didn't think I left that much of an impact on the local residents."

A hard lump knotted in the pit of her stomach. What a stupid mistake for her to have made. How was she going to talk her way out of this one? "Well—" She nervously cleared her throat. "—it was an assumption. I mean, you were at the party held in a mansion on Mercer Island, and it seemed that only the wealthy and socially prominent were on the guest list." She paused, hoping it would achieve the impression she wanted to project. "Or were you a party crasher?"

Hunt managed to suppress an amused chuckle. He had to admit a grudging admiration for her that extended beyond the obvious physical attraction. She had a quick mind and had neatly side-stepped the issue of her blunder and even made an admirable attempt to turn the tables on him. There was a lot more to her than good looks and the ability to pick pockets.

"A party crasher? Not at all. I've known the Swansons literally all my life." He took the last bite of his lunch then toyed with the stem of his nearly empty wine glass. As he downed the last swallow, he considered his options on how to proceed. "Gwen...what brought you from Chicago to Seattle? Was this a career move, or do you have family here?"

Her laugh sounded forced, as if attempting to appear

both casual and spontaneous at the same time. "Working as a server for a catering company is hardly an upward career move. However, it does allow me to set my own hours and work when I want to."

He cocked his head and raised a questioning eyebrow. "And you felt you had to move from Chicago to Seattle to accomplish that?"

His expression may have conveyed innocence, but Aurora caught the message buried in the depths of his green eyes that told a very different story. He wordlessly conveyed an obvious determination that said he did not intend to let the subject drop. Escalating anxiety welled deep inside her then rippled through her body. Her mind darted from one possible explanation to another trying to find just the right words to satisfy his questions without running the risk of alienating him or being caught in another blatant misrepresentation.

As much as he left her unnerved equaled how much she knew she needed to establish some kind of relationship with him if she was going to prove her father's innocence. Although she didn't yet know exactly how that was going to help her accomplish her goal, she instinctively knew it would.

"Obviously not." A nervous chuckle surrounded her words in spite of her attempt to suppress it. "I love the outdoors, being near the ocean and the mountains. Being from a large city, I also enjoy access to all those amenities rather than living in a small town—things like proximity to a major airport and cultural offerings such as museums, theater, and concerts. I have all of that here more so than anywhere else I've been. Chicago is certainly situated on a large body of water, but it's not the ocean. And the shoreline around the Chicago area doesn't include the mountains sloping into the water with the waves crashing on the rocks."

"Those same amenities are available in other major cities—" He tilted his head and shot a challenging look in her direction. "—such as San Francisco, for instance."

Was it her imagination, or was he baiting her? Why had he specifically mentioned San Francisco? Was it for the same reason she had mentioned Medina where he lived? "That's true, but Seattle had more of an appeal. Actually, it was the state of Washington I found desirable. California is so crowded and way too expensive."

"That's interesting. It sounds like you researched your move before you made it. You said you like the catering business because it allows you to set your own hours. Is that what you plan to have as your career? Maybe start your own catering company? Or is your plan to snag a husband?"

"What?" Her eyes widened. His question had caught her totally off guard, sparking a spontaneous flash of anger. "I didn't spend four years in college just so I could *snag a husband*!" She glared at him. "Marriage is not in my immediate plans."

He nodded his head knowingly as the wry grin tugged at the corners of his mouth. "I see…you're not husband hunting. Does that come from having already tried it, or do you have more important things on your immediate agenda?"

She took a calming breath as she tried to regain control of the situation. Anyone who said Huntington Wolfe III was a mindless playboy without any depth had never tried to match wits with him. He had just suckered her into admitting far more than she intended along with the added bonus of getting an emotional rise out of her. And she thought she had been on the alert and ready to handle anything he threw her way. She didn't even want to know what he would be able to do to a rival, how he could manipulate an unsuspecting adversary using nothing but words. To say she had merely underestimated him was a gross misstatement.

"Neither. I just don't happen to believe that marriage is the be all and end all. If I happen to meet the right man someday, then maybe I'll give it a try. But it's not a situation I'm consciously seeking out or concerned with."

Hunt extended his most sincere smile. "That's refreshing to hear, and in my realm of experience, it's also unusual." He had gotten the rise out of her that he wanted. College educated and a specific short-term goal. Definitely not someone searching for her place in the world and trying to figure out what she wanted to do with her life. Aurora Brentano had a definite purpose for being in Seattle while hiding behind a false identity. He had no doubts about her agenda being connected to her father's death.

Even though their conversation had been primarily verbal jousting—jockeying for position, an attempt to gain the upper hand—it had been a pleasant change from the type of women he usually encountered. They were quite often either social snobs who considered anyone without a family fortune and pedigree to be beneath them, that they were entitled to whatever they wanted, or they were gold diggers with dollar signs in their eyes.

And on the other side of the coin were the women he encountered in his investigations, usually those who were involved in the crime. Many of whom wouldn't give a second thought to doing away with whomever stood in their way. Aurora Brentano had turned out to be a breath of fresh air, a not very honest one at the moment, but a welcome change nonetheless. However, the jury was still out regarding her involvement with the thefts.

"So, how about you, Hunt? Have you ever been married?"

"Nope, I've managed to avoid that particular trap." He signaled to the waiter to bring him the bill. After paying it, he turned the conversation in an entirely new direction. "I had planned to take advantage of this beautiful day by going sailing for a couple of hours." He rose from his chair and held out his hand toward her. "Could I persuade you to join me?"

A moment's hesitation swept through her, followed by a quick flash of apprehension. Out on the water alone in a boat with the man she suspected of somehow being connected to her father's death, an invitation fraught with potential danger. Or was she reading something into it that wasn't there? Even though she was on alert, he had already manipulated her into saying more than she had intended. And now he had suddenly changed the subject and issued a social invitation. What was the real purpose of his invitation?

She forced a calm to her spiraling anxiety. She had blown it at the party. She couldn't take a chance on losing a second opportunity to get close to Hunt Wolfe. A third opening might never come her way, especially an opening initiated by him which would draw suspicion away from her personal plans.

"That sounds like fun." She returned his smile. "And it is a beautiful day for sailing. I have a few errands to handle, but I can put them off until tomorrow." She accepted his helping hand and rose from her chair.

A tingling charge of excitement rushed up her arm and immediately spread through her body. She withdrew her hand from his way too tempting touch as soon as she could without rudely jerking it away. Something darted through his eyes but disappeared before she could read it. Had he felt the same pull of heated desire as she did?

"Shall I follow you to your house so you can leave your car at home?"

"My car isn't here. I walked."

"Is there anything you need from home or are you ready to go sailing now?"

"Well, I would like to change clothes, especially my shoes. I need to put on something better suited to being on a sailboat. Why don't I just meet you there?"

"Okay." He jotted down his address and phone number on a napkin and handed it to her. "How about in an hour? Will that give you enough time?"

She took the napkin from his hand and stared at it. He had given her his home address. She knew exactly where it was from her middle of the night foray onto his property. "Is this a marina? What's the slip number for the sailboat?"

"That's my house"—a hint of a grin tugged at the corners of his mouth—"in Medina, not Hunt's Point. I have a private dock at my house where I keep my sailboat."

An invitation to his private dock. Definitely disturbing. No one to see her go out on the water with him. No one to know if she didn't return. And to compound the problem, she wasn't sure whether it was Hunt she didn't trust or if she didn't trust herself around this most desirable man.

"Yes, an hour will be fine. I'll see you then, Hunt." She turned to leave.

"I'm looking forward to it...Aurora."

She whirled around at the unexpected sound of her own name to be greeted by the unwavering gaze of his intense green eyes. A cold chill of pure panic ran up her back. Her mouth went dry. She swallowed several times in an attempt to keep her throat from closing off.

"What?" Her words came out as a breathless whisper. "What did you call me?"

He flashed a knowing smile as he turned toward the parking lot. "Aurora Brentano. That's your name, isn't it? See you in an hour."

Chapter Three

Aurora sat in her car across the street from the entrance gates of Hunt's estate. A quick glance at her watch said she was fifteen minutes late. In fact, she had almost changed her mind about showing up at all. The uneasy churning in the pit of her stomach told her far more than her conscious thoughts could. Was she about to be the sacrificial lamb heading into the lion's den? Or more accurately, presenting herself to a wolf in sheep's clothing?

How long had he known her true identity? Had he been on to her movements from the day she left San Francisco and arrived back in her hometown? And if so, why?

Uncertainty surrounded her scattered thoughts. She had to pull herself together. Their meeting at the waterfront café had obviously not been a coincidence. But beyond that? Was it possible that her father's death, while certainly not an accident as far as she was concerned, had no connection to the thefts? No connection to Huntington Wolfe III?

She sucked in a deep breath and held it for several seconds, leaned her head back, closed her eyes, then slowly exhaled. The calm she hoped for failed to materialize. Too many questions. Her only logical course of action would be to confront him and try to find out what she could without letting him suspect her true intentions, something she now realized would be more difficult than she originally believed. He had played her, proving himself extremely clever and adept. How many other people had been taken in by his playboy reputation and easy charm only to suddenly discover they were actually the prey when they thought they had been the predator?

She pulled her car into the drive at his estate, stopped at the closed gate, and pressed the intercom button. A moment later, Hunt's voice came over the speaker.

"Aurora...I was beginning to think you had changed your mind. Come on up the drive. I'll meet you at the front door."

Even the sound of his voice had an impact on her normally logical and rational way of dealing with adverse situations. The entrance gates swung open. She hesitated a moment. It was not too late. She could still back out of the driveway and leave. She clenched her jaw into a hard line of determination, then headed her car up the drive toward the large house.

The over-sized oak double doors with etched glass swung open, and Hunt stepped out onto the front porch just as she turned off the engine and climbed out of her car. A quick intake of breath and a racing pulse were her immediate reactions to the sight of him dressed in shorts and a sleeveless T-shirt. His long legs, broad shoulders, and muscular arms revealed a strong, athletic body. A golden tan attested to the amount of time he spent in the sun.

He closed her car door, then placed his hand at the small of her back to guide her toward the front door. "I was beginning to think I would have to track you down again with a third attempt at making a good *first* impression."

Aurora gathered as much resolve as she could muster while attempting to sound confident and in charge. "So, you admit you tracked me down. Our meeting at lunch wasn't a coincidence."

He extended a knowing smile. "Once again, guilty as charged."

She slowly shook her head as she gathered her thoughts and formulated them into words. "Could we move beyond this inane chit chat, shove aside these mindless pleasantries, and abandon whatever this game is that you're playing so we can get down to reality? You obviously know who I am. So, tell me why you're checking me out to the point of digging into my personal life? What business is it of yours? What are you looking for? What do you want from me?"

"So many questions. I wasn't aware I *wanted* anything special other than to know your name and how to get in touch with you. I wrote down your car license number when you drove away from the party in hopes of being able to locate you. But I must admit I was surprised when Charlie told me that Gwen York had just moved here from Chicago. That didn't agree with the California license plates on the car you were driving."

"And that was when you decided to invade my privacy?"

"I was naturally curious…" He flashed a sexy smile, one she suspected he used on numerous occasions in a calculated manner to influence a situation to his advantage. She stiffened her resolve. She had no intention of falling prey to his charms or letting him manipulate her in that manner—at least not a second time.

"You'd be surprised at how much information just a little bit of money can buy."

"I see." Even to her own ear her voice sounded nowhere near as firm as she wanted.

"Right this way"—he gestured down a hallway— "and out the back to the dock."

Out the back to the dock. The words bounced around inside her head, leaving a trail of uncertainty surrounded by a rapidly growing level of apprehension. Was he about to show his true intentions? Reveal the ulterior motive he had kept hidden?

She faced him. "Not so fast. You didn't answer my questions. I want to know what's really going on here. If you knew who I was, why did you play along with my subterfuge?" A quick shiver of anxiety darted up her back, and her throat tried to close off. "What is it you're after?"

"I think that should be my question, Aurora. With a college education and advancing in a good career in San Francisco, why would you return to your hometown under a false identity and get a job with a catering company serving champagne and hors d'oeuvres to society snobs?"

She eyed him skeptically. "You put yourself in that category of society snob?"

"No, I don't. In fact, my preference for those types of events is to RSVP with my regrets. If it's a charity function, I send a check as my donation. Attending was a last-minute decision. I find those functions boring and, for the most part, full of superficial pretentious people. I happen to like Carl and Eleanor Swanson. They're an exception to the superficial people rule."

His charming manner disappeared. "Now, back to my question." Suddenly, this easy-going playboy had become a force to be reckoned with—and all business. "Tell me, Aurora, exactly what are *you* after?"

At that moment, the only thing she wanted to do was get as far away from him as possible. She gathered as much resolve as she could. "Are you holding me here against my will?"

The surprised expression that darted across his face calmed her immediate concern. "Of course not. You're free to leave whenever you want to. All I asked was what you're after."

"I'm…uh, I'm not sure how to even respond to such a ridiculous accusation."

"Accusation? I wasn't aware I had accused you of anything. I simply took the facts presented to me and asked you to explain them."

Try as she might, Aurora couldn't come up with anything to get out of the uncomfortable situation. He apparently already knew quite a bit about her. She struggled to come up with some sort of fix for the awkward moment. Was the truth the best solution?

At this point, what did she have to lose? Maybe if Hunt believed he had the upper hand, he would let down his guard and give her some information she could use whether it implicated him in any wrongdoing or not.

She stared at the floor as she turned her options over in her mind. "All right, since you insist." She looked up, making eye contact. "I believe the police hounded my father to his death. There's no way he had anything to do with those thefts. I wasn't able to get anywhere with the man in charge of the case with phone calls from San Francisco, so I decided to investigate on my own."

Hunt fixed her with a penetrating stare. "Who did you talk to with the investigation?"

"I talked to several people. What is it you're wanting to know?"

Hunt carefully chose his words, each one specific and emphatic. "I want to know the name of the person you talked to, the man you said was in charge of the case. The man who wouldn't help you."

"I...uh...he said his name was Lt. Montrose. It's some kind of a multi-jurisdictional task force."

Nervous tension knotted in the pit of Hunt's stomach. Back in the days when Hunt had been responsible for separating wealthy people from their expensive jewelry, before detective sergeant Montrose had been promoted to lieutenant, he had been a real thorn in Hunt's side. He always believed that Montrose's hounding him was more personal than related to any evidence he may have had, whether flimsy, circumstantial, or viable—a theory attested to by the fact that Montrose never had enough proof to arrest him.

It was one of the reasons Hunt had decided to give up the cat burglar business, although a minor one. Not the fear of being caught, rather his boredom with devising new ways to frustrate Montrose by always staying one step ahead of him. Back in those days, Hunt had maintained one absolute rule he followed in determining which items to steal and from whom—never anything of sentimental value or family heirlooms. He dealt only in the gaudy baubles bought by ego-driven super-rich or the nouveau-riche who were anxious to impress everyone with their newly acquired wealth.

His problem at the moment? How to proceed with Aurora. It presented a tricky situation that would have him walking a fine line between necessary deception in order to know everything she knew without revealing his association with Excellence Insurance while at the same time wanting to help her resolve her obvious anxiety about her father's involvement and untimely death.

He had his own concerns about her father's guilt, suspicions that were not answered by the official police statement or what Lt. Montrose would have everyone believe. And his first skepticism dealt with the circumstances of Quentin's death.

Hunt quickly assessed his options then came to a decision about Aurora. "Let me help you."

Her eyes widened. "Why would you want to help me? This isn't some little problem like changing a flat tire, and it's certainly none of your business."

"This is something dangerous as clearly demonstrated by your father's death. I think you're in way over your head. You need help."

"So what is this?" Her entire attitude changed from cautious to aggressive and outraged. "Your way of showing off your macho? Being the big man? The knight in shining armor riding to the rescue of the foolish damsel in distress? I'm not some helpless little waif. I can take care of myself."

He heard her words, but her eyes told a different story. Wariness…anxiety…and a touch of fear. But fear of what? Of him? Of what the truth about her father might be? He wasn't sure. Maybe both.

"Never once did I think of you as some helpless little waif or a foolish damsel. I'm quite sure you're resourceful and can take care of yourself. I saw the way you lifted the wallet at the Swanson party. A neat and professional job."

"You saw that?" Her voice had lost some of its confidence. "Why didn't you say anything?"

He extended what he hoped would be a confidence-inducing smile. "To tell you truthfully, I was initially too shocked to say anything. After I recovered from my surprise, I was so impressed with your skill that I wanted to see what you'd do next. Imagine my further surprise when I watched you return the wallet to its owner with everything intact then turn down his one-hundred-dollar tip."

"And that's when you decided to delve into my personal life? To *spy* on me?"

"Spy on you? Don't be ridiculous. It's as I said. I wanted another chance to make a good first impression. That's why I made an effort to find you. Your sleight of hand was just additional incentive. I can honestly say I was stunned to find you weren't at all who you were claiming to be, that your true identity was Quentin Brentano's daughter."

Hunt brushed his fingertips lightly against her cheek, then tucked an errant lock of hair behind her ear. Her animosity, hostility, and suspicions seemed to suddenly vanish in a heated moment of intimacy. "And this brings us back to my offer to help you." He studied her features for a moment, including slightly parted lips that needed to be kissed long, hard, and often. "We'll figure out what's really going on and what the truth is about your father. I'll help you in whatever way I can. I have lots of resources available to me that you can't even dream of possessing. But for your part, you need to be prepared to accept whatever the truth turns out to be. Do we have a deal?"

"I still don't understand why you would be

interested in helping me. What's in this for you? What's your angle?"

"I take an interest in many different and unusual happenings that cross my path." He touched his fingertips to her lips to stop her from voicing the objection he saw forming in her eyes. "It was your mention of the difficulties you had with Lt. Montrose that sealed my interest in your situation. I've had a few run-ins with him in the past. He gets a notion into his head and pursues it as if it was fact even when he doesn't have a shred of evidence to support his personal opinion. I think there's a good chance that he did that to your father. I want to make sure he doesn't do it to you, too."

Then he smiled and put an end to that particular line of conversation. "So, do we have a deal?"

"Well…" Doubt and hesitation surrounded her utterance.

"Great!" He grabbed her hand and started toward the door leading outside. "Let's go sailing."

Aurora allowed herself to be led outside. There was no doubt in her mind that he had just deftly side-stepped the bulk of the issue and returned their conversation to more neutral ground. She would need to rethink her approach with him.

Maybe sailing was a good idea after all. He might let down his guard in a more relaxed atmosphere, something in his own comfort zone.

Hunt escorted her out to the large terrace. A pathway led across the lawn to his private dock. What little she had seen of the inside of the house between the front and the back doors definitely left her with the impression of not only an extensive fortune, but also good taste in furnishings and decoration. But as he had said, money bought lots of things—information, possessions, and even someone else to dispense good taste on his behalf. She inwardly flinched at the harshness of the words. It hadn't been a fair assessment.

"Here we are." The sound of his voice broke into her thoughts.

She came to an abrupt halt. To say she was surprised at what she saw would be an understatement. She had anticipated some sort of luxurious sailboat. She knew he owned a private jet and a seventy-five-foot cabin cruiser. She had assumed his sailboat would be on the same level of luxury. The size of the long dock dwarfed the little sailboat tied there. It was far removed from her expectations.

He held out his hand to assist her from the dock onto the sailboat. "Watch your step."

She hesitated a moment before accepting his help. The same potent arc of sexual energy leaped between them as had grabbed her when they were at lunch, once again catching her totally off guard. The breath froze in her lungs as she quickly withdrew her hand. His expression mirrored the strange feeling coursing through her body, an odd sensation she couldn't clearly identify other than it frightened her. Not physically but most assuredly emotionally.

Hunt felt it but didn't have a clue what it meant other than it left him slightly unnerved. He shook off the unwelcome impression. He had far more important things on his mind than a disruptive physical encounter with a desirable woman who looked like she belonged in his bed, but definitely the type who would also want a commitment in spite of her comments about not looking for a husband.

He finally forced out some words accompanied by what he hoped sounded like a casual chuckle. "Must have been a little bit of static electricity in the air."

"Uh…yes, I guess so."

They made eye contact. A long moment passed as each held the other's gaze. Hunt seldom found himself at a loss for words or in a situation where he didn't know what to do, but this had turned out to be one of those rare occasions. Aurora Brentano was an extremely tempting woman, both physically and intellectually.

But she represented a temptation he had to ignore if he intended to do his job. After all, business and pleasure didn't mix. At least not in this situation. Not until he figured out what this was all about—which pieces fit into the puzzle and which ones were nothing more than unnecessary clutter to be discarded.

He handed her a life jacket. "Here, safety regulations require that it be worn while out on the water." Then he put his on.

It took only a few minutes before they were under sail on Lake Washington. She had changed from the slacks, silk shirt, and sandals she wore at lunch to shorts, a plain cotton T-shirt, and canvas deck shoes. Breathtakingly beautiful. He didn't know how else to describe her except to add sexy, desirable, unsettling, confusing—and off limits. At least for the time being.

Hunt made a point of keeping the conversation light and casual without any mention of her father or the jewel thefts. But his mind kept working on a deeper level, attempting to sort out all the bits of information swirling around in his mind.

A sense of carefree abandon slowly replaced his anxiety. Skimming across the water under sail always invigorated him, leaving him momentarily free of responsibility for anything or anyone. His sixteen-foot sailboat was a small craft, easily handled by one person with minimal sailing skills, and not suitable for more than two people. Definitely not for any activity other than sailing. The brisk wind through his hair, the sun against his skin, the feel of the spray. It never failed to lift his spirits when he felt down or clear his mind when he had a confusing problem to decipher.

And his current problem of recovering the stolen jewelry for Excellence Insurance had a disturbing and unexpected side issue named Aurora Brentano.

Hunt motioned her over to join him on the bench seat. She hesitated a moment. Wariness darted across her face and settled in her eyes. Her body noticeably stiffened.

His gaze met hers. "Do you have any hands-on experience with a sailboat?"

"Not really. Actually, I've only been sailing two times before this. It was a much larger sailboat, and I was merely one of several passengers."

"This is a simple, one-person operation. It steers with a tiller attached to the rudder. I like to take it out on the lake when I need to think out a problem, usually early in the morning before the pleasure boaters get out on the water. It helps clear my mind of trivial matters so I can concentrate on what's important." He again motioned for her to sit next to him. "You seem to be nervous about something. Are you afraid of the water?" He shot her a questioning look. "Or perhaps you're afraid of me?"

"Nonsense." She took a deep breath, slowly released it, then sat where he indicated.

"Here." He grabbed her hand and placed it on the

tiller. "You steer for a while. Get a feel for it, how she responds to the touch."

A quick look of panic darted across Aurora's face as she jerked her hand away. "I can't do that. I don't know anything about it."

"No time like the present to learn. Sailing lessons are expensive." He flashed his best smile. "I'm willing to teach you for free. You can't get a better deal than that."

Aurora tentatively reached out and took hold of the tiller. Maybe the sailing lessons were free for the moment, but she was sure she would eventually be expected to pay…and not with money. She tried to dismiss the unwelcome thought by reminding herself that he had not made any improper advances, but the notion continued to linger in the back of her mind. When he questioned if she might be afraid of him…well, not exactly afraid but certainly wary. If he was somehow involved in her father's death, that made him a dangerous threat to her safety.

But for right now, she needed to keep him from being suspicious of her motives. And that meant going along with what he wanted for the time being—within reason. Hopefully, she wouldn't live to regret her decision. Or worse.

Much to her surprise, Hunt behaved like a perfect gentleman. He instructed her in steering, tacking, raising and lowering the sail, and even allowed her to bring the sailboat alongside the dock when they returned to his house. Even when the needs of sailing brought their bodies into physical contact as he showed her what to do, he made no attempt to press the advantage.

But gentlemanly? Definitely the last thing she had

anticipated of his behavior once they were in his sailboat out on the water. Piece by piece, he seemed to be tearing down her preconceived notions about him. Then the primary question again invaded her thoughts. Why would he be willing to go out on a limb to help her? What was in it for him?

After securing the sailboat, Hunt escorted her into the house. Without asking, he poured each of them a glass of wine. He paused before handing the glass to her. Reaching out, he gently brushed his fingertips across her cheek. "It looks like you didn't use enough sunscreen. You picked up quite a bit of red on your face, arms, and legs."

A tremor of apprehension was her only response to his words and his fleeting touch. Had the moment of truth arrived? Was this where he expected her to *pay* for the sailing lessons?

He withdrew his hand then gave her the glass of wine. "I don't know about you, but I'm hungry. Let's see what we can find in the refrigerator."

Once again, his abrupt change of subject caught her off guard. "Uh...yes, I am a little hungry."

He escorted her to a gourmet kitchen open to the den on one side. On the other side was a butler's pantry that led to a formal dining room. The kitchen had everything anyone could want, including a large island with stools for informal eating, wood-burning fireplace with comfortable seating arrangement for cozy atmosphere, and even a pizza oven. She had never been in such a lavish house so elegantly decorated as the little bit she had seen of Hunt's lifestyle. Normally, she would have felt uncomfortable and out of place from the moment she set foot inside the front door of a house like this. A place she couldn't wait to leave. But the only thing unsettling being the presence of Huntington Wolfe III.

"Ah…I was right." He stood in front of the open refrigerator door. "Some leftover poached salmon and dill sauce. I can add some vegetables and throw together a green salad to go with it. And if you'd like dessert, I think there's some cheesecake in the freezer as well as ice cream." He glanced at her, cocking his head to one side. "How does that sound?"

"Delicious." She couldn't stop the smile. Poached salmon with dill sauce referred to as *leftovers*. "Let me help. I'll make the salad."

They ate at the island in the kitchen. Dinner had a more relaxed feel to it, as if they had each decided to let down their guard a little bit. A hint of warmth slowly spread through her body. As much as she didn't want it to be so, she had to grudgingly admit that she genuinely liked him. But trust him? An entirely different matter.

After they ate, Hunt cleared away the dishes then poured them another glass of wine. He took her out onto the deck. The sky took on the hues of the approaching sunset.

Aurora evaluated the situation. The timing seemed right to take advantage of the more relaxed atmosphere and see what kind of personal information she could get out of him. "This seems to be a very large house. Do you live here alone?"

"I have a business associate who lives in the guest house on the grounds, but I live alone here in the main house. Why do you ask?"

She took a sip of her wine. That could only mean the person she saw on the balcony that night, the shadowy figure who jumped from the second floor to the lawn, was Hunt himself. "Just curious. You don't have a live-in housekeeper or household staff?"

"A staff of live-in servants…" The words seemed to be said more to himself than a response to her question. "That reflects my parents' lifestyle, not mine. I have someone who comes in once a week to clean, a gardening service that takes care of the grounds, a pool person who handles the swimming pool and hot tub, and access to a maintenance man who does miscellaneous repairs that I can't handle myself. But none of them live here and they certainly aren't on staff. I'm not really comfortable with a lot of people under foot, especially at times when I'd rather be alone. I do my own cooking, am capable of putting the dirty dishes into the dishwasher and running a load of clothes through the washer and dryer. If I'm having a party, I do what everyone else does. I call Charlie Gorman to cater it."

"The poached salmon and dill sauce was your doing?" She couldn't stop the surprise that surrounded her words.

He extended an amused smile. "And again—guilty. Cooking isn't that difficult. I used to date a woman who was a gourmet chef. I picked up several pointers from her."

"*Used* to date? What happened?" The words were out before she could stop them. Heat spread across her cheeks. Thank goodness for the sunburn to hide her crimson flush of embarrassment. "I'm sorry. I didn't mean to blurt that out. It's certainly none of my business."

"No harm. It ended over an ego problem. And in case you're wondering, it was her ego, not mine."

Yet another surprise. It seemed to be a

straightforward honest answer to a personal question. One thing became clear. She needed to get out of his house before he had her totally mesmerized and under his spell. She didn't have time in her life right now to entertain thoughts about a personal relationship regardless of how physically desirable she found him. A relationship with Huntington Wolfe III would be totally impractical. And possibly dangerous.

"The breeze has turned a little too cool for the way I'm dressed. That's probably a sign for me to head for home. Thanks for the sailing lesson. I really enjoyed it. And your leftovers made a delicious dinner." She rose to her feet. "I'll take my wine glass to the kitchen on my way out."

He stood up, took the glass from her hand, set it on the table, then pulled her into his arms. A moment later, his mouth was on hers. As if they had a will of their own, her arms ended up around his neck as her mouth fully responded to his kiss, a kiss that proved to be everything she imagined it would be. Undeniable passion curled her toes and left her wanting more. So much more.

It had all happened so quickly. Despite being on guard and alert to any untoward action on his part, she hadn't been prepared for such a sudden move without any warning. Or for the way her body responded. Somewhere in the back of her mind, a voice kept telling her to get out while she could. She tried to ignore it, but the voice continued to pound inside her head. It yelled at her, repeating over and over that her priority was clearing her father's name, not indulging her own desires with this totally unacceptable playboy.

Hunt finally broke the kiss. Aurora didn't know if she felt relief or disappointment. Possibly both. Her thoughts spontaneously escaped out into the open before she could stop them. "Why didn't you try that when we were on your sailboat instead of waiting until I was leaving?"

He brushed his fingers against her cheek sending a tremor of desire rippling through her body. "Because I didn't want you to feel pressured...trapped on a boat in the middle of a lake without a choice...unable to simply walk away as you can now."

Her earlier confusion had just doubled. It was the last thing she expected him to say. She had never met anyone like him and wasn't sure how to handle the situation.

Hunt saw it in her eyes and sensed it with her body language, the indecision and uncertainty. An awkward situation to say the least. As much as he wanted to pursue what he had started—what she had allowed—he had a larger goal to keep in mind. There was much more at stake than a physical relationship with a beautiful and desirable woman. At the moment, their alliance was built on tentative footing and deception. Something more akin to quicksand than solid ground.

Time to call it a day, to let her leave and make her believe it was her idea to walk away. To let her think she had control of the situation. He took a step back. "You're right. It's a little chilly out here. Let's go inside. I'll build a fire in the fireplace. Or..." He gestured down the deck. "We could warm up in the hot tub."

She turned toward the door leading back into the kitchen. "No, I really do need to leave. I have several things to do yet today. I..."

She picked up her empty wine glass and carried it inside. A combination of disappointment and satisfaction hit him. He had accomplished his goal of establishing a temporary liaison with her in order to gain information, but it had left him wanting something far more personal.

"I'll walk you to your car." He hurried to catch up with her. "How is your time tomorrow? I think we should get together and compare notes, figure out what the next step is."

"I think I can free up some time. Give me a call about nine tomorrow morning." She shot him a knowing look. "I assume you have my phone number?"

He couldn't stop the laugh that escaped his throat. "If I don't, I can assure you I'll have it by nine o'clock in the morning." Hunt walked her to the front door and watched as she slid in behind the steering wheel of her car. Then his gaze traveled down the driveway to the street and lit on the car parked across from his entrance gates. A car he had never seen in the neighborhood and certainly not parked in front of his neighbor's house.

A quick jolt shot through his body putting all his senses on alert. The house across the street was set back from the road same as his, only it didn't have the wall and security gate in front. A visitor would have logically gone up the driveway and parked at the house rather than on the street. He pressed the remote to open the entrance gates for Aurora at the same time as he grabbed his cell phone from his pocket and hit the speed dial for Johnny O'Brian.

"Get out the side gate and check the car across the street from my driveway. It could be someone tailing Aurora or watching my house. Either way, I don't want anyone following her home."

"I'm on it."

Aurora's car pulled out of the driveway and headed

down the street. The mysterious car had parked facing in the opposite direction. It immediately sped away with the headlights turned off. Hunt shook his head as he watched it disappear up the street into the darkness.

Chapter Four

Johnny grabbed two beers from the refrigerator, then seated himself at the kitchen island. He opened both bottles and handed one of them to Hunt.

He accepted the bottle, took a drink from it, then set it on the granite-topped counter. "Were you able to get a license plate number on the car or a clear look at the driver?"

"Zip. The license plate and surrounding area on the trunk and bumper were obscured with mud splatter even though the rest of the car looked like it had just been washed."

"I was highly visible on the front porch to anyone inside the car. I assumed the driver would focus his attention on me instead of looking for someone coming toward him on foot from around the corner of a stone wall." An amused chuckle escaped Hunt's throat. "Of course, you know what *they* say about someone who assumes…"

"Whoever was in the car definitely didn't want to be identified." Johnny took a swallow of his beer. "The windows were tinted too dark for me to be able to see the driver in what little bit of daylight remained. The only thing good was that Aurora turned out of the driveway and headed in the opposite direction to what the car faced. I watched the unknown car as it drove away. The brake lights never came on, and it didn't come back down the road, so whoever was behind the wheel didn't turn around. It's a long way up to the next cross street, so I doubt he would have been able to catch up with her car to tail her if that was his intention, assuming it was a man behind the wheel, and assuming he was the only occupant of the car. A lot of assumptions and no facts. Maybe if I had grabbed a night vision scope—"

"Don't worry about it. We'll know to be more alert from now on, especially since we don't know whether it's Aurora or me who is under surveillance. Or by whom." Hunt frowned. "Or exactly why."

Johnny took another gulp from his beer bottle. "Where do we stand? Did you get anything helpful from her?"

"Only a tenuous agreement to work together to figure out what's going on based on the assumption that her father was framed. There's that word *assumption* again. What we have is a tenuous agreement wrapped in a layer of caution, another layer of suspicion, and a final layer of deception—kind of like trying to walk on quicksand."

Hunt took a sip of his beer. "She's college educated and street smart with a quick mind—a formidable combination. Her stated intention is to clear her father's name. Probably true, but that doesn't mean there isn't more to her agenda. I offered to help her but didn't reveal my personal interest in the case and certainly not my involvement with Excellence Insurance. Since the police have already labeled her father as the thief and with Montrose in charge of the task force, there's no way she'll get any help through legal channels. Under those circumstances, the only sure way for her to clear her father's name is to identify the real thief and discover evidence to the fact. If she is involved in the thefts, that's going to be tricky to clear his name without revealing her own culpability. If she has an additional objective, she didn't let on.

"I'm sure she already has a list of suspects, and judging by a couple of things she said when we had lunch, she's already checked into my background, and my name probably has a prominent place on that list. One interesting tidbit—right after her father died in that crash, she had some phone conversations with Montrose. He basically dismissed her. She took an immediate dislike to him."

Johnny's robust laugh filled the room. "Well, at least we can give her points for that."

"She hasn't attempted contact with Montrose since arriving here and didn't tell him she planned to come to Seattle, so there's no reason for him to suspect she's on the scene." Hunt frowned as a thought struck him. "Unless he's been investigating her as Quentin's accomplice. Which takes us back to the mysterious car parked across from my front gate. It's possible that Montrose has me under surveillance just for old time's sake. But that wouldn't explain the obscured license plate or dark tinted windows. There's nothing subtle about Montrose. His style has always been *in your face*."

Hunt slowly shook his head. "Something's off. I can feel it in my gut. It's the same feeling I used to get when I cased a heist and everything was set to go, then I'd cancel it literally at the last minute. Something…I don't know what…something is out of whack here."

"That one job you decided to pass up, the one where you changed your mind as you were literally walking out the door… Your gut was one hundred percent right that time. It turned out to be a police sting. You never would have been able to talk your way out of that one. So, I say listen to your gut. It's never lied to you." Johnny cocked his head to one side and raised a questioning eyebrow. "Maybe you should consider installing cameras at the front and side gate and also at the dock in back."

Hunt nodded his head in agreement. "Yes, it looks like we need to beef up security to something more than just the main house and the guest house. I should have done it the morning after the intruder the other night."

After a few seconds of thought on the matter, he gave Johnny his decision. "I want security expanded to include the grounds, everything within the surrounding wall. Make sure there's no blind spots. Record everything twenty-four seven. Would you take care of installing the necessary equipment? I don't want to hire an outside company and make it known that I'm seriously increasing security."

Johnny nodded. "I'll pay cash for the equipment and do the installation myself so there won't be a paper trail for someone to find. I think I can place the equipment so it won't be visible to anyone approaching the gates or the dock. I'll set up monitoring in the guest house for me and also in your office. Do you want to be able to monitor things from your bedroom, too?"

"Yes, but make sure the monitoring in my office and bedroom isn't visible. Hide it inside some kind of cabinet that locks. I don't want a visitor to know it's there."

Hunt and Johnny spent another hour discussing the equipment and its placement then Johnny left.

Hunt retreated to his office. He grabbed the phone, paused a moment, then dialed Aurora's number. A slight chuckle escaped his throat. Yes, as she suspected, he already had her phone number. After a couple of rings, she answered the phone.

"Hi. It's Hunt. I'm just checking to make sure you got home okay."

"Why wouldn't I?" Caution surrounded her words, coming through loud and clear.

"Well…it's probably nothing, but, uh, did you notice the car parked across the street when you left my house?"

"Yes, is there something wrong?"

"I hope not, but it might be a good idea for you to keep a sharp lookout. Make note of any strange cars parked by your house, take down license numbers. Be aware of the people around you and try not to put yourself in a vulnerable position or questionable situation." He forced a chuckle he hoped would relieve some of the tension. "And don't go walking down any back alleys in questionable neighborhoods, especially at night."

"That, uh, that sounds like you think someone is following me."

"The driver could just as easily have been watching my house or me. And there's always the possibility that it was nothing more than a car parked there for a totally valid reason having nothing to do with either of us. But the car did leave as soon as you pulled out of my driveway. I didn't see anyone walk up to it and get in which means the driver was already sitting in the car. I think caution is in order."

They talked for a few minutes longer, then agreed to meet back at his house the day after tomorrow rather than the next day as originally planned. Hunt wanted the additional time so Johnny could get the new video equipment installed. Security for his house was already good but the grounds were another matter. After Johnny installed the added security, the entire property would be well protected. Anything they said or did at his house wouldn't be able to be monitored. At Aurora's father's house…well, anyone could have gotten in there and bugged it. He made a mental note to have Johnny do a sweep of her house looking for any listening devices.

Hunt retreated upstairs to his master bedroom suite comprised of three rooms. The sitting room consisted of a small sofa, wood burning fireplace, flat panel television, and bistro table with two chairs. From the sitting room, he entered his bedroom. It was an expansive room with king size bed facing the French doors that led to a balcony with a beautiful view of Lake Washington. The balcony was accessible from both the bedroom and sitting room. The décor was masculine without being so macho that a woman would feel uncomfortable. The large bathroom had a roomy walk-in shower with multiple spray heads, spa tub, and even a sauna.

He went straight to his huge walk-in closet that also contained a dressing room. Sliding back the panel behind the shoe rack, he worked the combination, then pressed the little finger of his left hand against the optical scanner before turning the handle to open the wall safe—a procedure more obscure than the commonly used right thumb or index finger. His original thought had been to put the safe in his office but finally decided the hidden panel in the back of a room inside another room on the second floor would be more secure.

Moving some papers and cash aside, he grabbed the clip-on holster containing the 9mm semi-automatic handgun and the ankle holster with the small 25 caliber semi-automatic. He methodically cleaned each weapon then unloaded and reloaded the magazines. Both Hunt and Johnny were licensed to legally carry concealed weapons, due primarily to the intervention of Excellence Insurance in the form of a request on their behalf.

A shiver of apprehension rippled through his body. One man—Quentin Brentano—was already dead. Accident or murder? Was it because of the man's guilt or was he an innocent man wrongly accused by a relentless and overzealous police detective? For a moment, he flashed on the Victor Hugo novel *Les Misérables* with the relentless Inspector Javert ruthlessly pursuing Jean Valjean. Whatever had gone on between Montrose and Quentin Brentano exceeded the simple risk of stealing jewelry.

****

Hunt leaned back in his chair and studied Aurora as she stared at the computer screen in his office. He shot a quick glance across the room at Johnny, then returned his attention to Aurora. She had been understandably wary of Johnny's presence at first but seemed to quickly accept it. What she had shared and added to his computer files represented an impressive gathering of information, especially for an amateur without the important contacts Hunt possessed.

Of course, she had been working on it for two months rather than the few days Hunt had been officially involved. She even had a list of everyone robbed and their addresses, exactly what was taken, its value, and who carried the insurance. It also explained her pickpocket venture at the Swanson's party, a means of confirming information without arousing suspicion by asking questions.

The main thing the three of them had accomplished that morning was to narrow down the list of suspects to a small handful. Even though neither asked, Hunt and Aurora each voluntarily provided information on where they were at the time of the various thefts. And with each having verifiable alibis for most of the dates, the uneasy alliance became more comfortable even though not totally trusting.

He refilled his coffee mug then held the carafe out toward her and raised a questioning eyebrow.

She placed her hand on top of her cup. "No more for me, thanks."

He looked at Johnny who also declined a coffee refill. After replacing the carafe on the warmer, Hunt swiveled around in his chair until he faced Aurora.

"So, what do you think? After you removed me as your prime suspect—at least I hope you did—we cut the suspects back to a short list of possibilities. At this point, the most obvious candidate is Charlie Gorman. He had access to all the locations both a couple of days before when he checked out the kitchen and the layout for the party, then the afternoon and night of the party including time after the guests left when his people cleaned up. And I've always been curious about how he manages to live beyond the income provided by his catering business, a rate of personal spending that even exceeds the outrageous prices he charges. Of course, Charlie defends his rates with the tried and true *you get what you pay for…you want the best, you pay the big bucks.* And his company is the best."

Aurora added some information. "I sure wouldn't rule out Stu Allen, Charlie's chef. I've noticed in the time

I've worked there that Stu made several three-day trips out of town, usually mid-week when there aren't any catering jobs. He claims he visits his sick mother in Arizona, but he could be fencing stolen goods, meeting with whoever decides what type of jewels will be stolen next, or three days would give him time to fly to Grand Cayman to make deposits in a numbered bank account in the Caribbean."

Johnny made a quick note. "I can run that down…find out where he goes."

Hunt added information about leads he had pursued. "I've checked into all the victims. None of them are having money problems, at least not to the extent that would lead to the desperate move of faking a theft in order to file a false insurance claim. There's been some gossip around the yacht club about a couple of the members who have had financial setbacks, but I didn't find anything serious enough for them to stoop to insurance fraud."

"Hmm…" A thought struck Aurora, something she hadn't paid any attention to at the time. "Charlie spends a lot of time on his cell phone. Not lengthy calls, just the opposite, usually less than sixty seconds, and almost all of them incoming. He's constantly making notations and sending information from his cell phone. I had assumed he was sending information back to his office computer about schedule changes and updating current bookings, but now, I'm not so sure. He even has a little black book where he jots down information. You know, the old-fashioned way with paper and pencil."

"We need to get a look at that notebook. It could be hard copy backup to the information he's sending from his cell phone." He wrinkled his brow into a slight frown.

"It would be helpful to know if he's super security conscious so that the information he sends from his cell phone is actually encrypted rather than merely protected by standard security software. It would also be helpful to know if he has everything synced and automatically sent to the Cloud as backup."

"The way he lives on that cell phone, he'd miss it immediately. But that notebook of his is a different tale. I can lift it without him knowing."

"We need to do something different than just taking it. We can't have him realize it's gone. Johnny loves electronic gadgets and has anything and everything as soon as it hits the market. He even has a couple of items that are still in the beta testing stage and not officially available to the public yet. One of his toys is a battery-operated palm-sized scanner. Not only does it copy and has the availability of transferring material to another device using a USB connection, it is Wi-Fi equipped and can send the information to a computer in a few seconds. We only need to get our hands on Charlie's notebook for a minute or two along with some privacy. Before you go to the catering office, Johnny can hack in and figure out how to get access to Charlie's office Wi-Fi."

Determination covered her face. "I can do it. Give me that scanner thing. I'll go to the catering offices on the pretext of checking the schedule for upcoming work."

Hunt gave her a hard look. "Are you sure? If he catches you, it could be dangerous."

She flashed a confident smile. "No problem. I just won't let him catch me."

Those may have been her words, but he saw the anxiety that darted across her features. His concept of them working together was to have her share any information she had with him and maybe bounce some ideas off her. It hadn't included her putting herself in danger. He was being paid a great deal of money for his risk. It was his job. He had the experience and training to take care of himself in dangerous circumstances. She would be exposing herself to a risky situation without the means of being able to defend herself if something went wrong. Yet she was willing to do it to clear her father's name.

To the best of his knowledge, no one in his dysfunctional family had ever put themselves out for another family member simply because it was the right thing to do, even when there wasn't any physical danger. If there wasn't something tangible in it for them, they couldn't be bothered. His relationship with his cousin, Rita, was the only exception to that reality. They had always looked out for each other.

His mind flashed to a time ten years ago when Rita lived in Portland, Oregon. She had been stalked by a former boyfriend who had become increasingly menacing to the point where she had become afraid of him and what he might do. The police said she didn't meet the requirements to get a restraining order.

Without consulting her, Hunt had packed her belongings in the middle of the night when she was out of town for the weekend, moved her to his house in Seattle, then he and Johnny had a *compelling chat* with the young man in question. They made sure he understood exactly how unhealthy it would be for him if he continued stalking Rita.

At first, she had been angry when she discovered what happened but soon dropped the tough façade and thanked him. Knowing she was safe was all the thanks he needed.

Hunt returned his thoughts to the problem at hand. "Johnny, would you take Aurora out to the guest house, give her that scanner gadget of yours, and show her how to use it while I take care of some business matters?"

"Sure thing, Hunt."

As soon as they were out of the main house, Hunt grabbed the phone and dialed Leo Jordan at his home in London. "Hope I didn't wake you."

"No problem. Do you have some good news for me?"

"Only that I'm making some progress. What I need from you is any information you can give me identifying numbered accounts in the Cayman Islands, specifically in the names of Charlie Gorman or Stu Allen." He paused a moment as a thought occurred to him. "You should probably add Prestige Caterers to those names."

"You do know that numbered Caribbean accounts in Grand Cayman are the same as the numbered accounts in Switzerland, don't you? They won't share any information with anyone."

"Yeah, I know it's a long shot, but if there's anything you can dig up through your international banking contacts, it could be helpful."

"I'll give it a try."

"One more thing. Is there any mention in the progress reports you've received about either Charlie Gorman or Stu Allen being considered suspects?"

"No, those names haven't crossed my desk. However, as a rule local law enforcement doesn't keep the insurance agency apprised of suspicions, only results. And sometimes not even that."

"What are the chances of Lt. Montrose granting a request to keep you in the loop on any leads and the investigation in general?"

A spontaneous chuckle escaped Leo's throat. "I'd say the chances are about as good as him keeping *you* apprised of his investigation, but I'll see what I can do."

They talked for a few minutes before terminating their conversation. By the time Hunt had dumped the remaining coffee and washed out the carafe, Johnny and Aurora returned from the guesthouse.

"Everything set?" Hunt's gaze darted from Johnny to Aurora and back to Johnny.

"No problem, Hunt. She'll handle the scanner just fine."

Hunt opened a desk drawer and handed her a cell phone. "Don't use your own cell phone anymore, not for any reason. Turn it off right now and keep it turned off until this is over. Use this one instead. It's disposable and was purchased with cash so it can't be traced. Give the number to Charlie. It's too suspicious for you to claim you don't have a cell phone, only a pager. You run into any problems at all, call me or Johnny. Our burner phone numbers are programmed into the phone I just gave you."

Aurora stuck the burner phone in her purse, turned off her personal phone, then shot a quick glance in Hunt's direction. She didn't like the look of concern on his face. It told her he was worried about her being able to handle the job. Normally, she would resent someone doubting her abilities, but she had to admit to a less than confident feeling about this one. She had volunteered to venture into unknown territory, putting herself in a dangerous situation. She assured Hunt she could handle the job. Her father was dead. Was she about to confront the person responsible?

"What kind of self-defense training do you have?"

Hunt's question intruded into her thoughts, catching her by surprise. "Self-defense training? You mean like judo or karate? One of the martial arts?"

"Not necessarily. I'm talking about basic self-defense. Maybe a course at the Y or a health club...something like that."

"Well...no, nothing like that. I exercise regularly, go to aerobics class once a week, and jog three or four times a week before work. But since I've been back here, I haven't done much more than exercising in the house."

He cocked his head and studied her for several seconds. "And you think that will protect you against someone with a gun or knife?"

Her eyes went wide with fear. "Someone with a gun?"

He headed for the office door. "Come on, we're going to the workout room. I'll show you a couple of basic self-defense moves. Nothing fancy, just something that will allow you to get away from an aggressor."

Hunt took her down the hall to a room obviously dedicated to exercise and workout. Mats covered the entire floor. In one corner was a rack containing weightlifting equipment. There was a stationary bike and other workout machines. It had everything a health club would provide.

"Okay. Let's start with a simple grab. You're walking along and someone comes up behind you. He puts one hand over your mouth so you can't scream, and the other arm goes across your neck to incapacitate you—like this." Without warning, quicker than she could follow his actions, she felt herself being grabbed by the shoulders and whirled around with her back to him. A second later his left hand covered her mouth, and his right arm stretched across her neck, just as he had said.

Helpless, vulnerable, and frightened. All the emotions hit her at once along with the clear reality that she didn't have a clue how to defend herself against such an attack. She struggled, trying to free herself from his grip. He shoved her against the exercise bike, pinning her there with his body by leaning against her back.

She attempted to hit at him only to discover that he had somehow managed to immobilize her arms at her sides. Her heart pounded and her mouth went dry. Gasping for breath, her throat closed off when she tried to swallow. A quick jolt of panic shot through her. Intellectually, she knew it was only a demonstration, he wasn't trying to hurt her. But emotionally, it felt so real. She managed to grab his arm and tried to pull it away from her neck.

As quickly as he had grabbed her, he suddenly released her from his hold and took a couple of steps back. "Now, do you see what I'm talking about, Aurora? I told you exactly what I was going to do, and you were still totally unprepared and unable to defend yourself. We're in a well-lit room inside my house, and I meant you no harm. Consider what it would be like if this happened in a dark parking lot at night with your attacker determined to get what he wanted by any means necessary. Then double that potential physical harm to life-threatening if he has a knife or gun. If you're going to pursue this line of investigation into your father's death, you need to know how to protect yourself.

Agreed?"

"I see what you mean." She put her hand to her throat where his arm had been, an involuntary action rather than a need to soothe any pain. "Okay, where do we begin?"

"You grab me the same way I grabbed you. I'll show you how to defend against it."

They spent the next couple of hours going over self-defense moves until Hunt was satisfied that she had a grasp on the basics. Next on the list—some last-minute instructions before Aurora's foray to Charlie Gorman's office.

****

Aurora slid in behind the wheel of her car, pausing a few moments to compose herself. She didn't know exactly how to describe the last couple of hours other than eye-opening. She had always believed that exercising regularly, being in good physical condition, was enough. Certainly, being aware of her surroundings went along with that and trying to avoid potentially dangerous locations. If on foot, don't take that short cut down an alley rather than staying on the sidewalk on a well-lit street.

Common sense combined with some physical self-defense techniques. I have to admit that was a worthwhile two hours.

Then the memory of the sensation of someone watching her flashed across her mind. Would she be putting her new skills to use sooner than she thought?

She started her car and drove to Prestige Caterers. Glancing around the parking lot with a newly aware eye, she pulled into an empty space next to a security light and in direct sight of a security camera. Charlie's car confirmed his presence in the building. She took a calming breath in hopes of settling her rattled nerves. This was for real, not part of a magic act performance or a game. She opened the front door and went inside. Pausing at Charlie's open office door, she knocked on the doorjamb to get his attention.

Charlie looked up. His face brightened when he spotted her. "Gwen…this is a surprise. What can I do for you?"

She walked casually across the room as she made a quick survey of his desktop. Her gaze lit on the small black notebook next to a stack of papers. A nervous tremor ran through her body. Telling Hunt that it would be an easy task might have been a bit too optimistic. Picking someone's pocket was one thing, but grabbing an item in plain sight without the owner noticing it was missing presented quite a different matter. And then she needed to get it safely returned to the exact spot where she had found it. How to accomplish the task—her mind darted from one possibility to another.

"I wanted to check the schedule for the next couple of weeks so I can get the workdays on my calendar." She extended a friendly smile. "I'm available for all the days you can give me. I need the money." She offered a shy smile, pretending embarrassment at having admitted a precarious financial condition.

He gestured toward the large schedule board that covered an entire wall. "Unfortunately, there doesn't seem to be too much going on the next couple of weeks." He indicated five bookings on the schedule. "You can put those dates on your calendar, and you know I'll give you first call if anything else comes in."

Charlie leaned back in his chair, his gaze slowly

traveling down her body then back to her face. His close scrutiny sent a ripple of discomfort across her skin, a far different impact than Hunt had on her senses.

"Did Hunt Wolfe manage to reach you? He called here wanting to know how to get in touch with you."

"Uh...yes." She leaned against his desk, purposely obscuring his view of the little black book. "In fact, he invited me to go sailing with him."

"Oh? Did you go?"

"Well...not yet." She definitely wanted to change the direction of the conversation. She slipped the notebook under her shirt and tucked it into the waistband of her jeans. "Okay if I use your little girl's room? I'll write down those dates as soon as I get back." She turned toward the door, then returned her attention to him as if she had just remembered something. "Oh...I meant to tell you. I have a cell phone now. I'll give you the number when I return." She feigned a half apologetic and half embarrassed smile as she eased away from his desk and hurried toward the hallway as if her bathroom visit had become urgent.

She locked the bathroom door, quickly scanned each page of the notebook into the device, and sent the information to Hunt's computer. A quick jolt of panic grabbed her as soon as she stepped back inside Charlie's office. Her heartbeat jumped, and her breath caught in her throat. A frown covered Charlie's face, and he seemed to be searching for something. His notebook?

"Did you lose something? Maybe I can help you find it." She leaned across the desk and in one smooth move *accidently* knocked the stack of papers to the floor as she unobtrusively inserted the notebook into the scattered pile. "Oh, no. I'm so sorry, Charlie. Here...let me clean up this mess.

"That's okay. This stuff was too close to the edge of the desk."

She began gathering the papers farthest away from where she knew the notebook was, leaving the majority of them for Charlie to sift through. Her muscles tensed as her nerves twisted into a knot. Watching from the corner of her eye, she saw him *discover* his little notebook among the scattered papers. She also saw the look of relief on his face that said he hadn't attached any suspicion to the incident.

The same sense of relief flooded through her, accompanied by a soaring exhilaration from the excitement. The potential danger. The possibility of being caught.

They replaced the papers on his desk, then she took a pad from her purse and jotted down the catering dates. Before leaving, she gave him the number of the disposable cell phone. She smiled. "Be sure to call me if you schedule any new catering dates."

"Sure thing, Gwen."

Aurora exited the building as casually as she entered, making sure there was nothing rushed about her appearance while her heart continued to pound in her chest and the adrenaline surge refused to subside. A block away from Prestige Caterers, she pulled into a grocery store parking lot, turned off the engine, leaned back, and closed her eyes.

She breathed an audible sigh as if she had been holding her breath. A grin turned the corners of her mouth, then grew into a broad smile that quickly turned into a jubilant laugh. The thrill of successfully pulling off the caper continued to dart around inside her, a much different sensation than merely picking a pocket.

Her body suddenly jerked to attention. An unnerving awareness hit her…again. So many times, she had shoved the uncomfortable sensation aside but always to no avail. She had even tried to figure out some common thread for when and where it happened. The only thing she had come up with was the fact that she felt safe inside Hunt's house, but everywhere else left her feeling vulnerable. Should she tell Hunt about it? It was a question she couldn't answer. Once again, she forced the awkward moment away and continued on to Hunt's house.

The emotional high continued to churn inside her as she drove through the gates at Hunt's estate. She charged into his office. "Did the transfer come through okay?" Her words came out in a breathless rush. "I didn't have time to verify anything. When I got back to Charlie's office, he had already missed the notebook. I barely got it returned before he became suspicious."

His laugh in response to her question put a sudden stop to her elation.

"What's so funny?" She frowned. It felt as if he had thrown cold water on her accomplishment. "Did I screw it up? Did it transmit gibberish?"

"Not at all. You were perfect. Everything came through nice and clear. I'm laughing at what the information in his little black book told us."

"I don't understand." She cocked her head and stared at him, confusion replacing the excitement of just moments ago.

"We now have a logical explanation for all of Charlie's phone calls and how he's able to live above his catering business income."

She couldn't control the hint of irritation that crept into her voice. "Are you going to keep me in suspense, or do you plan to share the information some time this century?"

"Charlie Gorman is running a bookmaking operation."

"He's a bookie?" Her laughter joined his as she slowly shook her head. "I never saw that one coming." Then she sobered. "Of course, now that we know he doesn't have any objection to participating in illegal activities, does that make him a more likely candidate to be our jewel thief rather than removing him from our list?"

Chapter Five

Hunt studied Aurora with a critical eye. As soon as the high from her successful excursion to Prestige Caterers wore off, she had claimed a corner of the couch in his office and hadn't moved. That was an hour ago. He sat next to her.

"What's wrong? You seem disturbed...or maybe just distracted. Did something happen at Charlie's office that you haven't mentioned?" An errant thought popped into his head, and to his surprise, he found it upsetting. "Did that jackass make a grab for you?" He couldn't keep the edge out of his voice. "He seems to think it's his right and privilege to grab the female employees' ass whenever the mood strikes him. One of these days he's going to find himself slapped with a lawsuit—if he's lucky. Or looking down the barrel of a gun in the hand of an outraged boyfriend if he's not."

Aurora dropped her gaze to the floor as her brow wrinkled into a frown. Hunt had become a master at being able to read people. It had only been a couple of days since they agreed to collaborate, only a couple of days since they had gone sailing, but he had picked up on the downcast eyes and wrinkled brow as the trait that told him she was considering what to say. It wasn't a matter of her not knowing how to answer a question or that she was formulating a lie, only that she was considering holding back on some things—actually, no different than he was doing.

She looked up. "There is something…"

He instantly recognized the wariness in her voice and the uncertainty in her eyes. He steeled himself against any outward show of emotion. "A problem?"

"Well, it's probably nothing. Just my imagination."

He placed his hands on her shoulders. "Tell me." He felt the tension in her muscles. No question that she was mentally wrestling with some sort of problem. "What's wrong? Did something happen?"

Aurora slowly shook her head. "As I said, it's probably nothing. But I've had the feeling that someone has been watching me ever since I arrived from San Francisco and moved into my father's house. I haven't really seen anyone, but it's like a tickle at the back of my neck." She rubbed her hand across her nape. "It became more frequent and intense since the morning after we went sailing. Maybe it's only a reaction to you telling me about the car that night, but it feels a lot more real than just my imagination playing tricks on me, especially the last couple of days."

"You haven't seen anyone? No strange cars parked in front of your house? Seeing the same person in several different places?"

"No, nothing like that. It's the sensation of someone's stare boring into the back of my head, but when I turn around, I don't see anything out of place or unusual. It doesn't really have a threatening feel to it, but it is disconcerting."

Aurora watched the emotion flicker in the depths of Hunt's eyes, but she couldn't read the meaning or intent. A cold chill ran up her back. The deeper she dug into the jewel theft case that had somehow ensnared her father, the more tenuous her hold on the situation and the more unsure she was of everything where she had once been so certain.

And on the top of that list resided Huntington Wolfe III. He had been her prime suspect before she had contact with him, and now, he had slipped to the bottom of her suspect list. She still wasn't sure what the truth was, but with each passing hour he seemed to be less a threat and more an ally.

But imagined or real, the anxiety continued to lodge in the pit of her stomach. It picked at her consciousness saying someone was watching her. The police? Someone who had dealings with her father? Someone involved in the jewel thefts? There was even a possibility that Hunt had someone watching her, but why? To protect her or spy on her? She didn't seem to be able to get a firm grip on anything, including her own trepidation. That lack of control left her rattled and her nerves frayed.

And Hunt...before she left his house following their afternoon of sailing, he had kissed her with a heated passion that melted her insides like butter on a hot stove. He left her wanting more and, at the same time, frightened of her desires. Then, to her surprise, he had not made a repeat advance, and she didn't know why. Neither of them had mentioned it. But that didn't stop the sexual tension that crackled in the air whenever they were together. She couldn't speak for him, but she most assuredly felt it.

Just a few months ago, her life had been in control and running smoothly. She liked her job in San Francisco and had made many friends since moving there. Then suddenly her father was dead, and she found herself in an uneasy alliance with the last man she ever thought would have a connection to her life. And now, she had to deal with the decidedly uncomfortable sensation of an unseen presence that left her unsettled and concerned.

"Is there any security equipment or an alarm system at your father's house?"

"None that I'm aware of. It's a middle class, low crime neighborhood. Mostly families. Very quiet. Never any problems."

"Are you sure you'll be okay there?"

She mustered a confident smile. "Of course." She glanced at her watch. "In fact, I should be going there now. We've had a busy and productive day, but my brain is refusing to process any more information. Besides, it's almost dinner time, and I'm sure you have other plans for the evening."

"Not a thing on my calendar for tonight. Let's go out to dinner. Some place casual with live entertainment. A change of pace from all this concentrated effort." He projected an upbeat attitude, she suspected more to ease her concerns rather than what he actually felt.

"You don't need to do that…to take me out to dinner."

"Of course I don't *need* to, but I want to. I'll follow you to your house so you can leave your car, then we'll go from there. That way you won't have to drive home from my house later this evening."

She made one more feeble attempt to object, then Hunt won her over. As he followed her toward Bellevue, he called Johnny. "Aurora and I are going to dinner. There's more than just the car parked across from my driveway the other night. She says she's had a nagging sensation that someone is watching her but hasn't spotted anyone. While we're eating, I want you to sweep her house for bugs. I'm going to get her permission to install a security system, even if it's only to alarm the doors and windows so anyone trying to break in will be greeted by a loud siren." He disconnected from the call as she pulled her car into the detached garage at her father's house. He parked across the street and turned off his engine.

Of course, another way to resolve the problem of her safety, assuming she was actually in danger, would be to have Aurora stay at his house until they identified the jewel thief and uncovered the truth about her father's death. But that presented a very real problem. He wasn't sure he could handle that much temptation, even with her staying in a guest room on the ground floor and him upstairs. He tried to shake away the concern as he unhooked his seat belt.

A shadowy figure emerged from the bushes at the side of her house. A hard jolt of adrenaline pumped through his veins. With her back to the intruder, she had no way of knowing someone was approaching her. Hunt leaped out of his car and charged across the street at a full run. His heart pounded. His breath came in hard gasps as he gained speed. He had to alert her to the danger even if it meant scaring away the intruder.

"Aurora...behind you!"

The sound of his voice stopped the stranger in mid stride. A moment's hesitation, and the shadowy figure retreated around the corner of the house and out of sight. Hunt made the split-second decision to go to her rather than following a shadow into the darkness. He was not armed, but the intruder might be.

A moment later, the roar of an engine reached his ears, then the sound faded into the distance as an unseen car sped down the back alley. The look of fear on

Aurora's face told him he had made the right decision.

Her entire body trembled as he pulled her into his arms. She clung to him like someone grabbing for a lifeline. He forced his breathing into a slower mode. He didn't want to add to her obvious anxiety.

"Are you okay?" He nestled her head against his shoulder as he caressed her back, all the while scanning the surrounding area for anything or anyone that seemed out of place.

"I…yes, I'm…"

He held her tighter, trying to ease the tremors coursing through her body. "Did you get a glimpse of whoever it was? Notice anything that might help with an identification?"

She pulled in a deep breath, then slowly exhaled. "I'm sure it's nothing. Maybe someone lost? Wanting to ask for directions—"

"Stop it! Don't do that." His stern tone cut into her words, matching the determination churning inside him. "Don't even try to dismiss this as *nothing*. I saw it. No one walking down the sidewalk. No one spotting you getting out of your car and wanting to ask for directions. Someone had been hiding in the bushes at the corner of your house and came up behind you. This was someone lying in wait for you to come home. Most likely the person you felt watching you."

He placed a tender kiss on her forehead. "Somebody knows who you are, knows you're here and not in San Francisco. Do you have any guesses who that might be? Maybe someone from San Francisco who knew you were coming here? Does that ring any bells?"

"I can't imagine who it would be. I didn't tell anyone in San Francisco where I was going or about my father's death. I put in for a leave of absence, saying I had some personal family business to handle. I haven't run into anyone I knew when I lived here. The only people I've had any real contact with are those at Prestige Caterers, you, and Johnny. So, unless someone I knew spotted me on the street or was a guest at one of the catered parties…"

She shook her head and wrinkled her brow into a slight frown. "But even if someone did recognize me, it doesn't make any sense for that person to sneak up on me from a hiding place in the bushes. Or to run away when you shouted."

Hunt released her from his embrace, then placed his hands on her shoulders. "Pack a suitcase. You're staying at my house until we figure this out."

There was no mistaking the conviction in his voice or the look of absolute authority that covered his features, clearly visible in the illumination from the streetlight. He left her no room for any objections. She didn't know if she felt relief at the decision being taken out of her hands or irritation with him for telling her what to do without bothering to ask. This time, however, her rattled nerves told her she was thankful not to have to make the decision.

"While we're inside your house, don't say anything. Just pack a bag and bring it out to my car. Okay?"

"I don't understand—"

"We'll talk about it on the way back to my house."

They entered her house, and she went to her bedroom to pack a suitcase. A quick look around told him how easy it would be for even an inexperienced culprit to break in. While she gathered some of her belongings, he went back outside and called Johnny.

"Someone was at Aurora's house hiding in the brushes waiting for her to come home. She's inside now packing a bag. I'm bringing her back to stay in the guest room. Do you have enough equipment to install an alarm system at her house tonight? For now, only the doors and windows with a silent alarm that alerts each of our cell phones."

"Yes, I can get that done. Do you want me to wait until you get home, or should I grab my things and head that way now?"

"Do it now. I'll explain it to her on the way back to my house. I still want you to sweep for bugs, but if you find any, leave them in place. I don't want whoever it is to know we're aware of what's happening. See if you can trace the signal back to the receiver or at least get a serial number and find out who bought the equipment." He disconnected from the call and went back inside. A minute later, she returned to the living room, suitcase in hand.

He saw through her attempt at putting up a brave front, her expression far removed from calm and confident. They silently left with Aurora locking the front door, then they went to Hunt's car and drove away.

"Did you pack enough for a few days...just in case?"

She forced a weak smile. "Yes, although I'm not sure this is really necessary."

He ignored her comment. "Did you pack a swimsuit to use in the pool and hot tub? Just because the circumstances are not what you anticipated doesn't mean you can't enjoy the amenities."

A tinge of red flushed her cheeks as she lowered her gaze to the floor. "Yes, it did occur to me to add my swimsuit."

As they drove to Medina, Hunt told her about adding the alarm to her house. The objection he anticipated seemed like nothing more than a token effort than anything real.

Hunt glanced in the rear-view mirror. He spotted the car behind him moving up closer and closer. His muscles tensed as he gripped the steering wheel. "Is your seat belt fastened tight?"

Her gaze darted to him, then to the passenger side mirror. "What's going on?"

"I'm not sure. Maybe nothing." He made sure to observe the proper speed limit, using his turn signal when changing lanes and turning corners, staying back the proper distance from the car in front of him. He even circled a block to see if the car would follow. It stayed with him.

"Well, let's see how serious you are," he mumbled toward the rearview mirror.

Using his turn signal again, he pulled into a grocery store parking lot, then into a well-lit parking space by the grocery store's front door. He pulled out his cell phone as if making a call but used it to snap a series of pictures of the car pulling in behind him. Both the driver and passenger got out of the car and started toward him. After snapping pictures of the two men approaching the rear of his car, he immediately sent all the pictures to his computer, and as a precaution, he also sent them to Johnny's computer and phone.

Lt. Dan Montrose knocked on Hunt's car window and motioned for him to lower it. A quick glance toward Aurora's side of the car brought Detective Roger Whitcomb into view. Roger had been Montrose's partner for about five years. This wasn't the first time Hunt had been stopped on the streets and harassed by them.

"So, Hunt…" As always, Montrose oozed arrogance from every pore, even calling Hunt by his first name. "Out for a little drive? Who's your friend?"

"Well, well…if it isn't the ever popular and always charming Lt. Dan Montrose." When Hunt turned toward the passenger side of the car, he noted the narrowing of Aurora's eyes when he identified Montrose. He gestured toward Roger. "And his faithful sidekick, Detective Roger Whitcomb."

Hunt returned his attention to the lieutenant. "If you hadn't been tailgating me to the point where I felt I needed to get off the street to avoid a potentially dangerous traffic situation, you could have followed me all the way home. Of course, that would necessitate you crossing the line from Bellevue into the Medina police jurisdiction. And you know how the Medina police feel about jurisdictional interference."

"And I repeat, who's your friend?" He stared at Aurora. "You have some identification?"

"No, officer. I don't have any identification on me." She offered up a friendly smile. "Since I'm not driving, I didn't find it necessary to bring my purse."

"You gonna make me ask a third time?" Montrose's attitude turned aggressive, and his voice demanding. "What's your name?" He straightened and moved his hand toward his holster in a threatening gesture.

Hunt saw the scowl of disapproval cross Roger Whitcomb's face. He addressed his comments to Montrose, making no effort to hide his contempt for the lieutenant. "I don't know what you think you're trying to do here, but I'm sure the Bellevue police won't be happy to hear that you've been harassing innocent people on their turf even to the point of threatening to draw your gun." He gestured toward the grocery store windows. "Be careful of your next move. You seem to have attracted the attention of some onlookers. The Bellevue police aren't any happier about jurisdictional interference than the Medina police."

"Hunt..." Aurora lightly touched his arm as she interrupted him, drawing everyone's attention to her, "I don't want to be the cause of a rift between you and your friend." She directed her conversation to Montrose. "My name is Gwen York. I'm a friend of Hunt's from Chicago. I'm considering a move to Seattle, and Hunt has been nice enough to show me around. Is there some problem with that?"

"Gwen York." He said the words more to himself than to anyone. Then he whirled around and headed for his car.

Hunt called out the window toward Montrose's retreating form. "In case you lose me at a stoplight—" A slight grin tugged at the corners of his mouth when the lieutenant shot him a scornful look. "—I'm heading to my house. And if it has somehow slipped your mind, I live in Medina, just up the road a bit."

As soon as Montrose moved his car out of the way, Hunt backed out of the parking space and exited the parking lot. He watched in the rearview mirror as the unmarked police car sped off in the opposite direction with tires screeching.

"So, that's the Lt. Montrose I talked to from San Francisco?"

"Yeah, the one and only. A real charmer, isn't he!"

A hint of a grin pulled at her lips. "Based on my

telephone conversations with him, he's everything I thought he'd be." She extended a questioning look at Hunt. "What do you think that was all about?"

Hunt wrinkled his forehead into a frown. Lots of thoughts darted through his mind, including all the times the lieutenant had hassled him over the years. While some of the accusations were true, Montrose had lacked the proof to back them up. Most of them were nothing more than harassment. A clear-cut case of abuse of power. A situation where someone with Hunt's financial means, social standing, and powerful connections could easily take it up the chain of command, causing a lot of trouble for Montrose. But shining the spotlight on himself was not in his best interest, so he chalked it up to being an inconvenience with nowhere for Montrose to go with it. He did, however, take pleasure in baiting Montrose to see how far he could push him.

"It's just the lieutenant flexing his ego and arrogance. We've had more than our share of clashes over the years. The only thing that keeps him moderately in line is the reputation of my attorney, Frank Tanner, and the fact that I have the financial means to keep him from pushing me around. He's the type of cop who gives a bad name to all the honest, hardworking officers who put their lives on the line every day." Hunt clenched his jaw in determination. "But that doesn't mean he should be written off as a fool. He's definitely an ass, but he's not a fool."

They continued to Hunt's house. As he pulled into the garage, he glanced toward the guest house. His gaze landed on the older, non-descript car Johnny used when he was watching someone and didn't want to be noticed. It was the answer to a problem that had circulated through his mind since Montrose confronted them in the parking lot.

Aurora needed a car. It was impractical to believe she could be restricted to his house unless she was with him or Johnny. She needed something to drive. In her own car, she ran the risk of Montrose spotting her and running her plates for identity confirmation. Or equally possible was the lieutenant already having a description of Aurora Brentano's car and license plate number with orders for him to be contacted if anyone spotted it.

The same problem existed if Hunt gave her one of his cars. Montrose undoubtedly knew the make, model, and license plate of everything registered to Hunt. The lieutenant would stop her, and she would be forced to show a driver's license. He could rent her a car, but that created a paper trail.

Johnny's surveillance vehicle would be perfect. It was registered to Hunt's corporation at Frank Tanner's law office address. Non-descript on the outside including some dents, scrapes, and in need of being washed. But the inside was a different story—in perfect mechanical condition including a powerful new engine and all the latest electronic gadgets.

Hunt settled her into one of the four ground floor guest rooms. A silent sigh of resignation told him he would much rather have taken her suitcase upstairs to his bedroom. It also told him any intimate contact with her could only lead to trouble. If his only objective was to help her as he had claimed, if he didn't have a business arrangement to recover the stolen jewelry, things would be different. But that wasn't the case. He had to keep everything in its proper perspective. He had a job to do and that had to come first before any personal considerations.

His priority at the moment was to get his mind off the personal and back on business. "As you said earlier, it's dinner time. All things considered, I think it's better if we stay here rather than venturing out tonight, especially with Montrose on the prowl. Just because he has no authority in Medina doesn't mean he's not watching my house."

"You're right. I got away with saying I didn't have any identification on me. But if he had insisted on searching your car, he would have discovered my purse where I shoved it under the seat. That would have told him what he wanted to know and put our activities under a magnifying glass."

She scrunched up her mouth as if thinking about something. "Could he have been following you from the time we left your house? If so, he would have my license plate number and know where I live. By now, he would have checked both of them and know I'm Quentin Brentano's daughter."

Aurora looked up at Hunt, locking her gaze with his for several seconds before saying anything. "How much of an obstacle is he going to be in searching for the truth about my father's death?"

Hunt turned her question over in his mind. Her unwavering stare left him slightly rattled. Keeping his hands off her was proving to be a lot more difficult than he first thought, although he knew from day one it wouldn't be easy. "He's the one who was fixated on your father as being guilty. And he's the one who was chasing your father when the car went over the cliff. I'd say that makes him a major obstacle no matter how you look at it."

Even though he had initially dismissed the idea, could Montrose have been the one parked across from his house that night? One fact kept bombarding him. Aurora Brentano's presence had definitely compromised his investigation. His job for Excellence Insurance had suddenly become twice as difficult. It had inadvertently been relegated to the back burner. And he wasn't sure exactly how he felt about that.

As if he had no control over his own actions, he wrapped his arms around her and pulled her into his embrace. A moment later, his mouth was on hers. The kiss they shared the day they went sailing had continued to linger in his mind. Keeping his hands off her during the ensuing days had proven more than merely difficult. But standing in front of her house, holding her as he'd attempted to provide comfort and soothe her rattled nerves after the shadowy figure ran off, stretched his good intentions to the limit.

The kiss deepened, her response as enthusiastic as it had been the last time. She tasted of sweetness and earthy passion, a tantalizing combination he found impossible to resist. He slipped his tongue between her parted lips, twining the texture with hers. His labored breathing increased, a match for each ragged breath she took. One thought continued to assault him. He had to stop this before it was too late, before they ended up in his bed.

With great reluctance, he finally managed to break off the kiss. He cradled her head against his shoulder and rested his cheek against the top of her head. The silken strands of her hair trailed across his fingers.

"As you said, it's dinner time." A huskiness clung to his words.

And a single thought continued to circulate through

his mind. What would happen after dinner, later that evening when it was bedtime? He'd told her she would be safe at his house from the danger surrounding them. Was she now worried whether she would be safe from him?

****

As Hunt and Aurora finished dinner, Johnny returned from installing the alarm system at her house. He did a quick survey of the kitchen island. "That looks good."

Grabbing a beer from the refrigerator, then a plate and fork, he joined them without waiting to be invited. The house rule said if the meal was served in the kitchen, everyone was welcome.

Hunt refilled Aurora's wine glass, then his own. "Everything go as planned?"

Johnny took a swallow of his beer. A slight frown crossed his brow. "As far as the installation, everything went smooth. I did a routine sweep for bugs. Didn't find any. As I was leaving, a car pulled up in front of the house next door, but no one got out. I couldn't swear to it, but I think it was the same car that had parked across the street here."

Hunt looked at Aurora, noting the alarm covering her face. "That's not good. If it's the same car, that means whoever was here had been following you rather than surveilling me and whoever it is knows where you live. But we don't know if it was the same person I saw at your house a little while ago."

He returned his attention to Johnny, his mind darting in a thousand directions at once—considering the possibilities, weighing the odds, determining a course of action. "Did you stick around to see what the driver would do?"

"I circled the block, but when I got back, the car was gone. It was just pulling up to the curb as I stepped off the porch so the driver saw me leaving the house. The alarm didn't go off, so whoever was in the car didn't try to gain access."

"I don't like that. The same car in both places means someone has made a connection between Quentin Brentano's house and me." Hunt leveled a serious look at Aurora. "The next question is whether this someone has gone a step farther and added you into the equation."

Aurora added her thought. "Could that someone be Lt. Montrose?"

Hunt took the last swallow of his wine, then set the empty glass on the counter with a combination of controlled anger and determination. "We're not getting anywhere. We can't sit here speculating about all the possible *what ifs*—"

The ringing of his primary cell phone interrupted. Even though Hunt, Johnny, and Aurora had all agreed to keep their cell phones turned off and use only the disposable phones, Hunt had decided to keep his turned on but leave it at his house. Anyone tracking his phone would think he was home.

Hunt checked the caller I.D., but the number was blocked. It rang a second, then a third time before he answered it.

"Wolfe? It's Roger Whitcomb. I need to talk to you."

"Well, you've got me. What do you want to talk about?"

"Not on the phone."

"I'll be here all evening."

"No, it has to be somewhere else, someplace we won't be seen."

Something about the detective's tone set Hunt's senses on full alert. "Why the conditions? I'm certainly not Montrose's favorite person, but—"

"Just you and me…and the woman who was with you."

"Gwen?" His heartbeat jumped into high gear. Extreme caution had just become the word of the day. "Why her?"

Hunt hesitated as he ran all the possibilities through his mind, including that notion that Aurora was the target, and this was the only way they could figure how to get at her without causing suspicions.

"I need to meet with both of you in private. It's urgent."

"I'm willing, but you can forget about Gwen's presence. That's not going to happen."

"Two hours. Discovery Park at the lighthouse. Both of you."

Before Hunt could respond, the call disconnected. Even though Roger's words were rushed, his voice remained steady without any indication of alarm.

Aurora broke into his thoughts. "What was that about? Who wants me to be where?"

Hunt checked his watch. Two hours didn't give him much time to come up with a plan. "It was Roger Whitcomb. He wants to meet with us in two hours. He didn't say what was on his mind, but whatever he wants, he seemed adamant about meeting with both of us, not just me. And apparently without Lt. Montrose. Roger refused to come here, insisting we meet in an out of the way place."

Johnny quickly jumped in with his opinion. "He's Montrose's partner. No way can you trust him. This is some kind of a scam—a trap. They're trying to set you up for something. Get you alone then it turns out you need an alibi for something. They'll refuse to give you one, which leaves you twisting in the wind."

Hunt slowly nodded. "It's a strange and unexpected turn of events, that's for sure. And what you said is a distinct possibility."

Johnny took another swallow of his beer. "How do you want to handle it?"

"It will be just you and me. I'll meet with Whitcomb, and you'll record it and at the same time send it live back to my computer, yours, and Frank Tanner's with an embedded time code. Aurora will stay here behind secure locked doors with the video surveillance turned on."

"No way!" She jumped to her feet. "It's my father's death we're investigating. I'm not sitting here, staying safely in the background, while someone else does what I should be doing." The look of determination covering her face said as much as her words.

And again, Hunt reminded himself that recovering the stolen jewelry was his primary objective, in spite of the fact that he seemed to be spending more of his time involved with Aurora's goal of pursuing the truth of her father's death. Their individual goals were obviously intertwined. At least he firmly believed that to be the truth even though he wasn't sure of the exact nature of the connection.

Hunt stared at the floor as he evaluated the options. Anxiety and confusion surged through his body, a situation he had seldom encountered. He wasn't sure which one had the upper hand, the anxiety or the confusion.

He looked up, his gaze moving from Aurora to Johnny, then back to Aurora. "Johnny, you leave now and find a place to stake out the meet location. Make sure you have room to maneuver around the lighthouse area without being seen since we don't know exactly where he'll be waiting. If he calls with any changes in plans, I'll call you."

"No problem. I'll grab my equipment and get going." Johnny checked his watch. "That will put me in place an hour before your scheduled arrival time."

Johnny ran down the path to the guest house. Five minutes later, he drove out the side gate used by the gardeners.

Hunt stared at Aurora for a moment. "Do you know how to use a gun?"

"Do I know how to shoot? You bet I do. Handgun, rifle, shotgun...take your pick. My father taught me to shoot about the same time as he taught me how to pick pockets. The only thing I have a little bit of a problem with is bow and arrow."

A teasing grin tugged at the corners of his mouth. "Well, if there's a call for any Robin Hood types, we'll excuse you from the auditions." He replaced his grin with a serious look. "Wait here. I'll be right back."

As she watched him hurry out of the room, her mind turned to fond memories from her childhood. A warm feeling settled over her, spreading a sense of calm to her tautly stretched nerves. Her father had taught her to pick pockets when she was twelve years old, at the time when she had started helping him with his magic act. It was also the same time when he taught her how to shoot and proper safety procedures in handling a gun.

She had continued to work as his assistant until she graduated from college and accepted a position with a company in San Francisco. It had been a ten-year period of fun in her life, a time when she and her father had grown very close. A time when they needed each other following the death of her mother when she was eleven years old.

Hunt hurried upstairs, went straight to his closet, and opened the safe. He removed the 9mm and the 25 caliber weapons, grabbed a couple of spare loaded magazines, and returned to the kitchen where he'd left Aurora. He wanted to make sure she clearly understood the parameters of what he was about to do. He placed the 25 caliber gun in an ankle holster on the island.

"I'm licensed to carry a concealed weapon, know all the safety precautions, and am deadly accurate. Same with Johnny. I assume you're not licensed. You wearing this will be breaking the law. We're going to be meeting a police detective. Do you understand the implications of that?"

"I do, and I'll take my chances."

"This ankle holster is probably going to feel a little awkward at first, but your jeans will hide it from view. When we get there, I want you to stay in the car. If it becomes necessary for you to get out of the car, keep your distance from me. That will initially make it more difficult for someone to cover both of us. I'll most likely be the primary target. If any shots are fired, get yourself to cover as quickly as possible. And remember, Johnny will also be at the location—hidden from view."

She took the ankle holster from him, withdrew the handgun, checked the magazine, then loaded a round in the chamber and set the safety. Pulling up the right leg of her jeans, she strapped it to her ankle, then lowered the denim leg to cover it.

As she stood up straight, she cocked her head and shot Hunt a questioning look. "Can you see it?"

"Nope, no indication at all." He clipped the 9mm holster to his jeans at the small of his back, then pulled his shirt over it."

He hesitated for a moment before speaking. "I'd feel better if you stayed here."

"He said he wanted to meet with both of us. And you seem to keep forgetting that it's my father who was killed, which makes me very much involved. If he has some information to give us about my father, I want to be there."

"We don't know what he wants. He wouldn't say, which means it could be trouble. As Johnny said, it might be a trap."

"But why would he call if he didn't have some information to share?"

"Thus, Johnny's suspicions."

She shot him a curious look. "If you suspect a trap, why are you determined to go?"

Hunt didn't have an answer for that.

"We probably need to be going." He glanced at his watch. "It's still early enough that we might hit some traffic going across town. I don't want to get there too early, but I don't want to keep Roger waiting, either. I don't want to take a chance on him deciding we're not going to show up and leave."

Aurora started toward the laundry room to go out the side door into the garage.

"Wait." A ripple of anxiety assaulted his senses.

Was he being paranoid? No. Just exercising common sense that said to be cautious. "I want to check the street before I open the garage door and let anyone watching the house know that someone is about to leave."

It could all be nothing. Or it could be a colossal coincidence, although he didn't really believe in coincidence. But until he knew who had been watching his house, who had been at Aurora's house, and why Roger Whitcomb wanted to meet with him in an out-of-the-way location, he wasn't taking anything for granted.

He turned off the light in the foyer and also the porch light before opening the front door. He stared down the driveway into the dark. The illumination that came from the streetlight, combined with the security lights at the entrance gates, did not reveal anything out of place.

The next morning was trash pickup day. The neighbors across the street had their trash barrels at the curb in the same place they always left them, nothing suspicious about that. The gardeners had set his trash barrels at the side gate before they left that afternoon just as they did every week. There weren't any out-of-place cars in sight.

He stepped across the threshold onto the porch, Aurora right behind him. In an attempt to stop her from getting ahead of him, he held out his arm to block her path as he swept the surrounding area with a sharp eye. Everything appeared normal, yet a nagging tingle of anxiety told him otherwise.

A ripple of trepidation continued to assault his senses. A moment later, he stepped off the porch.

"Wait a second." Aurora bent down to adjust the ankle holster.

"What's wrong?" He turned to see what she was

doing.

And a fraction of a second later a shot rang out. The bullet ripped through his jacket. A sharp sting hit his upper arm just below his shoulder, a shot that would have caught him in the middle of his chest a second earlier before he turned toward Aurora.

A sharp adrenaline surge charged through his body. He instantly dropped to the ground, pulling Aurora down with him. He covered Aurora with his body. His heart pounded in his chest, the sound reverberating in his ears. A second then third shot in rapid succession shattered the night air of the normally quiet neighborhood.

Hunt reached for the 9mm snugged into the small of his back.

Chapter Six

Aurora held her breath as she tried to assimilate what had happened. Then Hunt's voice came at her, controlled and decisive, interrupting her thoughts. "Stay low. Get inside the house, shut the door, call 911, then call Johnny and tell him what happened."

She attempted to swallow her fear. "Are you—"

"Do it!" It was definitely an order, not a suggestion or a request.

She crawled inside the house on her hands and knees, closing the door so no one could see inside but not to the point where it clicked shut. Hunt would be able to get inside without reaching up to the door handle. Then she made a dash for the landline phone in the kitchen. Taking a calming breath, she tried to steady her rattled nerves. With trembling fingers, she called 911. As soon as she reported the shooting, she hung up. Next, she called Johnny using her disposable cell phone.

"Someone just shot at us."

"Is anyone hurt? Where are you?"

She heard the control in Johnny's voice, the same in-command confidence Hunt always displayed. And somehow it helped calm her. "I'm okay and Hunt seemed all right. We're at the house."

"Where's Hunt?"

"Outside. He ordered me inside the house and told me to call 911, then you. I don't know what…" Then she spotted the blood on her jacket. A hard jolt of fear assaulted her senses followed by an audible gasp. She had not been shot. The blood could only have gotten there as a transfer from Hunt. "Oh, my God! No!"

"Aurora? What's going on?" Johnny yelled into the phone, still controlled but with a touch of anxiety added to the calm of a moment earlier.

She tried to settle her rattled nerves, to ward off the fear welling inside her as she blinked away the tears forming in her eyes. *Stay calm. Hunt needs to know he can depend on me, no matter what the situation.* "There's, uh…there's blood on my jacket, but I wasn't hit. Hunt…I don't know what he planned to do. The last thing I saw was him reaching for his gun while telling me to get inside and call 911."

"I'm on my way back right now. Stay inside the house and away from the windows. Just in case, find something you can use as a weapon. In the kitchen—"

"I have Hunt's ankle gun."

"I'll be there as quickly as I can."

The line went dead as Johnny disconnected from the call. She put the cell phone in her pocket then stared at the blood on her jacket. It was as if she had become frozen to the spot. A sick churning in the pit of her stomach tried to work its way up her throat. Why would someone be trying to kill Hunt? Then another thought lodged in her mind, one that sent a second jolt of fear racing through her body. What if the shots were meant for her? What if she was responsible for Hunt being wounded? But who? Why? What if—

"Are you okay, Miss?"

The strange voice startled her out of her thoughts. Her body stiffened as she jerked to attention. Her first inclination was to reach for the small handgun strapped to her ankle, then her gaze focused on the uniform of the police officer.

"Where's Hunt? Is he all right?"

"He's on the front porch talking to my partner. We wanted to call the paramedics, but he's refusing medical treatment. Are you okay?"

"Medical treatment?" Panic jolted through her body and crept into her voice.

She bolted toward the front door, brushing the policeman aside as she charged out of the kitchen. When she yanked open the door, a wave of relief swept through her. Hunt stood on the porch talking to a policeman. Other than the blood surrounding the rip in his jacket, he appeared to be uninjured. "Hunt? Are you... Are you okay?"

"Gwen, please wait inside. I'll be there in a minute. Meanwhile, I'm sure the officer wants to take a statement from you."

"Your arm..."

"It's nothing, just a scratch. A little bit of antiseptic and a bandage...I'll be good as new. No need for you to be concerned."

Everything about him projected calm, control, and confidence. He called her Gwen. Obviously, he didn't want her revealing her true identity to the police. She knew the drill—keep the story simple and straight forward with as few specific details as possible. She turned around and found the other policeman standing in the doorway listening to the conversation.

Her panic subsided with the immediate physical danger seemingly gone, but it had done nothing to lessen her trepidation. She tried to run a scenario through her mind, something to tell the officer that wouldn't contradict whatever Hunt might have told the other policeman.

She returned to the kitchen with the officer. He seated himself at the island and took a notebook and pen from his shirt pocket. "Let's start with your name and address."

"My name is Gwen York, and I guess you could say this is my address for right now. I'm from Chicago and planning a move to Seattle. I'm staying in Hunt's guest room until I find a place to live and get settled."

"Guest room? That would be the guest house on the property?"

"Uh…no. I'm staying in one of the guest rooms on this floor here in the main house."

"Does anyone else live here? Servants? Relatives?"

"No one else lives in the house, at least not to my knowledge. There's a business associate of Hunt's who apparently stays in the guest house from time to time."

"A business associate? What's their connection?"

"I don't know. You need to ask Hunt about that."

"You said this associate *stays* in the guest house…stays there off and on when he's in town or lives there on a permanent basis?"

"I don't know. Again, you need to ask Hunt that question." Was it her imagination, or were the officer's questions not relevant to the situation at hand? She understood the need to know if there were other people in the house or who had access to the property, but why was he asking her rather than the man who owned the house? And more to the point, it was her understanding that the Medina police already had that information about their high-profile residents.

Knowing the people coming and going made it easier to protect the people living there. They would know about someone living in the guest house as a permanent resident. But she hadn't been an ongoing guest, hadn't even spent one night there yet. She was an unknown stranger as far as the police were concerned.

"Tell me what happened here, Miss York."

Aurora wrinkled her brow into a frown as she pursed her lips. "I'm not really sure. It all happened so fast. We walked out the front door, and someone took a shot at us. We hit the ground, then there were more shots…I think two more, but I couldn't swear to it. I have to admit I was pretty rattled. I've never been shot at before. Hunt told me to get back inside the house and call 911. And the next thing I knew, you were here asking me if I was okay."

"You retreated inside the house, but Mr. Wolfe didn't seek out a safe location?"

"He told me to stay low, get in the house, close the door, and dial 911."

"And what did Mr. Wolfe do while you were calling for help?"

"I don't know what he was doing. I was inside the kitchen on the phone, and he was on the front porch when I came inside."

"Why didn't you stay on the line with the 911 operator rather than hanging up?"

"I…" She slowly shook her head hoping to convey the idea that she was attempting to remember exactly what had happened. "I don't know. I guess that's when I noticed the blood on my jacket and panicked."

It was an odd question at best. It almost had the feel of an accusation rather than a simple question. Or perhaps it was her guilty conscience, the result of withholding information and lying to the policeman. Anxiety flitted across her skin, accompanied by a knot in the pit of her stomach.

"Did you see or hear anything? A car? Voices?"

"Nothing. It all happened so fast and was over so quickly. I'm sorry I can't be more helpful." A shiver darted across her skin. She hugged her shoulders as if warding off a chill. "I've never been shot at before. It's a frightening experience."

"Is there anything else you'd like to add?"

"I can't think of anything."

"Here's my card." The officer placed it on the countertop. "If anything else occurs to you, give me a call."

Hunt entered the kitchen, followed by the other officer.

Aurora rushed to him. She reached out toward the bloody slash in his jacket sleeve. "Are you sure you don't need to go to the emergency room? You might need stitches or at least a tetanus shot." Her initial panic had calmed, but her feelings continued to bounce between her concern for Hunt's injury and her discomfort about the nature of the officer's questions.

Hunt grasped her hand and held on to it, giving a little squeeze of reassurance. "It just grazed me. My jacket got the worst of it. And as far as a tetanus shot, I had one a couple of years ago when I was working on my boat and cut myself."

One of the recessed ceiling lights, a small one over the laundry room door, flickered for a couple of seconds then went out. The officer who had been questioning Hunt pointed toward it. "Looks like the bulb just burned out."

Hunt glanced at the light. "You're right. I'll need to replace it." Hunt casually took two wine glasses from a cupboard and set them on the island top, then turned his attention toward the two officers. "This has been an upsetting experience. Gwen and I are going to have a glass of wine to calm our nerves. Would you like to join us?"

The senior officer answered for both of them. "We're on duty, Mr. Wolfe. Thanks anyway."

Hunt poured two glasses of wine and handed one of them to Aurora. Then he turned his attention to the two officers again. "You've taken our statements, roped off my front porch along with the surrounding area, and said the crime scene technicians are on their way. Is there anything else you need from either of us? I'd like to tend to my arm if there's nothing more. It's starting to throb."

"Well, Hunt. I hear you had a little problem here tonight." Lt. Montrose strolled casually into the kitchen. He gestured back toward the front door. "The crime scene boys are here. They told me where to find you."

Hunt eyed the lieutenant, barely controlling his disdain. "You're a little bit out of your jurisdiction, aren't you? I don't appreciate having you invade my home uninvited."

"This is a crime scene."

"The crime scene is outside, not in my kitchen. And it belongs to the Medina police," he gestured toward the two officers acknowledging their presence, "not the Seattle Police, which forces me to ask what the hell you're doing here."

"I just happened to be in the area when I heard about the shooting."

"And where's your sidekick? Did you leave him on the porch to provide totally unnecessary *supervision* of the crime scene unit?" It had been a calculated question. Roger Whitcomb couldn't be in two places at once, and they were supposed to be meeting him in Discovery Park at the moment.

"We're off duty. I assume he's home."

"Well, lieutenant, unless you have *official* business here, you're not welcome in my home. If you don't leave my house immediately, I'll register an official complaint against you for trespassing." He gestured toward the Medina police officers. "And I have proof in the form of two valid witnesses."

Hunt watched as the conflicting emotions darted across Montrose's face. Unless the senior officer on the scene invited the lieutenant to stay, Montrose had no option but to leave. And what seemed on the surface to be nothing more than a drive-by shooting incident hardly warranted asking for assistance from another police department.

Montrose addressed his comments to the two officers. "If there's anything I can help you boys with, just let me know. The Seattle P.D. is always happy to lend a hand."

The senior Medina police officer instantly replied, "We don't require any outside assistance, Lieutenant. We're more than capable of handling our own jurisdiction. And the property owner has also made it clear that he does not want your presence."

Montrose leveled one final hard look at Hunt and slowly sauntered toward the front door, barely hiding his irritation and anger over being summarily dismissed and ordered off the property, a direction backed by the officer in charge of the scene.

Hunt glanced at the kitchen clock, then at the officers. "Is there anything else you need from us tonight?"

"No, Mr. Wolfe. Not at this time. We'll increase our patrol in this area for the rest of the night. Thank you for your cooperation."

"Fine. I'll walk you out." Not only did he want the officers out of his house, he wanted to make sure Montrose got all the way off his property without taking any unauthorized detours to check out the grounds. He shot a quick look at Aurora then at the laundry room as he escorted the two officers to the front door. He shook their hands. "Thanks for your prompt and courteous attention. Give the Chief my regards." Hunt returned to the house, leaving the crime scene technicians to pack up.

Aurora had not been aware of the small light over the laundry room door until it began to flicker. It obviously meant something to Hunt. As soon as the officers were out of the house, she hurried to the laundry room then slowly opened the door. The room was empty. But there was another door leading from the laundry into the garage. She cautiously approached it, then spotted something she hadn't noticed before—a peep hole of the type usually found in front doors. Why would anyone need a peep hole between the laundry room and the attached garage?

A shiver made its way up her spine, but it had nothing to do with the air temperature. She reached toward the door handle, then quickly withdrew her hand. Her heartbeat jumped.

Nothing to be afraid of. After all, there's police

officers on the premises, and Hunt is nearby. So why were her muscles tensed and her nerve endings drawn into a tight knot? Her hand trembled slightly as she reached toward the door again.

"You look like the heroine in one of those gothic novels."

Aurora's heart leaped into her throat, and her breath froze in her lungs. She whirled around and found herself staring at Hunt's teasing grin.

"Don't *ever* sneak up on me like that again! You just scared the hell out of me." She took a deep breath in an attempt to start her heart again. "What do you mean by gothic heroine?"

"You know the scenario. Everyone who has gone through the mysterious door in the gloomy old mansion has disappeared off the face of the earth. But that doesn't matter because whatever happened to everyone else couldn't possibly happen to the feisty heroine. She's determined to discover for herself exactly what's there regardless of how dangerous that decision would be, and she doesn't bother to let anyone know what she's doing or where she's going."

His expression turned serious as he crossed the laundry room to her. A moment later his fingers brushed her cheek as he looked at her with a questioning expression. A tingle of excitement rippled across her skin. "Only now...maybe the heroine uses some discretion, common sense, and caution? Maybe now she isn't so eager to do something that foolish?"

Her breath caught in her lungs, but this time it wasn't from fear. She finally managed to force out some words. "What was that business with the flickering light?"

"That was just Johnny letting me know he was back. He obviously came in through the gardener's gate, saw the police were still here, signaled that he was on the grounds, then went to the guest house to avoid being questioned."

Strange. Very strange. Hunt and Johnny seemed to have a well-oiled working relationship that functioned more akin to a detective situation than anything that could be considered *normal business*. Exactly who was Huntington Wolfe III? Shallow playboy with a family fortune who was dedicated to partying? She had already seen through that façade. But was there another dimension to him beyond a man willing to help her, even if his primary motive was to thwart Lt. Montrose in what was apparently a long-standing feud between the two men? And what about Johnny O'Brian? Exactly who was he? What did *business associate* really mean?

She wanted some honest answers but wasn't at all sure how to ask the questions. Or, for that matter, which questions to ask.

The door to the laundry room opened and Johnny walked into the kitchen. "Everyone's gone. What the hell happened here?" He gestured toward Hunt's bloody ripped jacket. "How's your arm?"

"It's nothing, just a scratch" He emitted a soft chuckle. "But it ruined my favorite jacket." Hunt took off his jacket, wincing a little as he maneuvered his arm out of the torn sleeve. "We were getting ready to leave to meet Whitcomb. I wanted to check the street first before opening the garage door and alerting whoever might be watching the house. One step off the front porch and someone took a shot at us. Grazed my upper arm. The other two shots slammed into the wall by the door. Hopefully, the police are chalking it up to a drive by shooting, even though this isn't a neighborhood where that happens. If not, then it's logical for them to assume I'm the target. After all, Gwen here has just arrived from Chicago and doesn't even live in the area."

"That's not going to hold water for long." Johnny's frown said as much as his words. "And what was Montrose doing here?"

"He said he was *in the neighborhood* and heard about the shooting. I don't know what he was really doing. I asked him where his partner was, but he just brushed it off, saying they were off duty, and he assumed Roger was home."

Johnny furrowed his brow into a frown. "This is the second time today that Montrose has been face-to-face with Aurora. It won't take much digging to figure out who she really is—if he doesn't already know. He probably already has a copy of the Medina police report even though the ink hasn't even had a chance to dry yet."

"What about the surveillance cameras?"

"I checked the recordings while waiting for everyone to leave. There's nothing on them that identifies the assailant. It looks like the shots were fired from behind the neighbor's trash barrels across the street. They're in perfect alignment with your driveway and front door. The shooter took off running down the street with his back to the camera.

"There was some activity about fifteen minutes before the shooting. A vehicle drove up the street, then came back down the street slowly. The license plates, both front and rear, were covered by something. A few moments later, the shooter ran into the camera line of sight from down the street and hid behind the trash.

Again, his face was turned away from the camera, almost like he knew it was there. About ten minutes later, he fired three shots from behind the trash barrels, then ran back the way he had come."

Hunt nodded. "Well, in case there was any question about it being a planned attack or merely a drive-by shooting, that pretty much erases the uncertainty. But it doesn't get us any closer to who or more to the point why."

Aurora unfastened the ankle holster and placed it on the counter, then addressed her question to Johnny. "What happened at Discovery Park? Was Roger Whitcomb there?"

"His car was parked near the lighthouse with someone sitting behind the wheel, but I couldn't get close enough to confirm an identification. Assuming it was Roger, that put Montrose here on his own. Roger couldn't have been in two places at once."

Aurora heard Johnny's words, but her attention became riveted on Hunt's arm just below the shoulder. Without the jacket covering the wound, it looked worse than he had originally led everyone to believe. A lot more blood, certainly more than the insignificant *barely more than a scratch* he had professed. She tentatively touched his arm. "You're hurt more than you claimed. It looks like you need stitches."

He wrapped his hand around hers and drew it away from his injury. "I'm fine. Honest."

Johnny interrupted the look that lingered between Hunt and Aurora. "What do you want to do about the meeting with Whitcomb? Do you want to make another try for it? He might have decided to wait to give you extra time."

"No, not with Montrose on the prowl. And the Medina police said they will have their patrol cars checking this area more often tonight. We're better off staying in and putting a new plan of attack together tomorrow. Even if Roger doesn't hear about the shooting on the news, I'm sure Montrose will tell him about it. Maybe knowing why we weren't there will push Roger to try for another meeting…assuming it was legitimate rather than a trap. Now, I'm more curious than ever about what he could want with us that he apparently chose not to share with Montrose."

As Johnny headed for the door, he pointed toward Hunt's wound. "Take care of that. I'll see you in the morning." He disappeared through the laundry room into the garage.

Aurora started to speak, but Hunt stopped her before she could say anything. "Don't tell me about my arm again. I've got some antiseptic and bandages upstairs."

"I'll help you."

He grasped her hand, gave it a little squeeze, and led the way upstairs while still clutching her hand in his. There was something very comforting about his touch, as if he was reassuring her that everything would be okay. Who was this man who seemed to have so many faces? He was definitely hiding something. But in spite of that, she truly believed she could trust him.

Hunt led her through the door into his master suite. She had tried to visualize what his personal inner sanctum would look like, but what she saw nearly overwhelmed her. Even in a house so filled with anything and everything anyone could want in a home, it almost took her breath away.

They went straight to the bathroom where he opened

a cupboard and took out a bottle of peroxide, some cotton balls, antiseptic, and bandages. Then he pulled off his shirt, again wincing as he stretched his injured arm over his head. She quickly and efficiently tended to his injury. Once she had cleaned the wound, she realized it wasn't as bad as she had originally thought. She applied the antiseptic and a bandage.

The sensation of his bare skin, his hard muscles, his nearness—everything about him excited her senses more than any man she had ever known. And it wasn't just a physical attraction, either. There was something special about him.

In addition to his intelligence, humor, and quick mind, she now felt the sense of trust, loyalty, and dependability he conveyed—all admirable qualities having nothing to do with his good looks and physical presence. Yes, she was definitely attracted to him on all levels. But what about Hunt? She had not seen any evidence of there being a woman currently in his life. If there was, surely, he would have insisted she stay at a hotel rather than his house when it became obvious that she couldn't continue to stay in her father's house, not with someone having been hiding in the shadows by her own front door. And if he didn't have anyone special in his life, well…

She tried to clear her mind of the thoughts, dangerous thoughts leading her in a direction that could only end one place.

"Aurora?"

The sound of her name snapped her out of the inappropriate place her mind had taken her. She looked up at him, at the honesty showing in the depth of his eyes.

"You looked like you were a thousand miles away."

He took her hand, then slowly pulled her into his embrace. "Is something wrong?" A quick chuckle escaped his throat as he glanced at his bandaged arm. "Other than the obvious problem of someone shooting at us."

His words came out as a soft whisper across her ear. She felt so safe and secure in his arms. She had tried to put the trauma of the evening behind her, to convince herself it was just a coincidence, nothing more. And even if it wasn't really a coincidence, it was only a minor incident. Just a warning and certainly not a death threat.

At least, that's what she wanted to believe.

But a warning about what? Lying to herself wouldn't make the lie a reality. The truth clearly said that someone had purposely shot at them. What was the shooter's true intention, to scare them or to kill? A cold shiver rippled up her back.

"Why would someone shoot at us?" she asked. "Does this have to do with my father's death? Is it possible… I mean, could there be a remote possibility that he really was somehow involved in or knew something about the stolen jewelry?" She rested her head against his shoulder, closed her eyes, and slipped her arms around his waist. "None of this makes any sense to me." She blinked away the moisture forming in her eyes. "I'm scared, Hunt. I don't understand what's going on."

The sadness and emotional pain in Aurora's words grabbed Hunt as nothing else ever had. She was close to her father, the kind of family relationship he had never known. She believed in her father, the man who raised her following her mother's death. The man she looked up to, admired, and respected. And now, she was being forced to question the true character of that man. It was obviously tearing her apart. And then to have someone shoot at them...

It had suddenly become vital for him to discover the truth about Quentin Brentano's death and determine whether he had anything to do with the jewel thefts. Even if it meant stalling his arrangement with Excellence Insurance to recover the jewelry. After all, these robberies started five years ago. What difference could another week or so make?

He held her tighter. She felt so good in his arms, as if she belonged there. He lowered his face to hers, capturing her mouth with a kiss, tender at first but quickly escalating. The passion he had been holding in check refused to be restrained any longer. He flicked his tongue across her lower lip, then slipped it into the dark recesses of her mouth. Her soft moan reverberated through his body, feeding into his growing excitement.

In spite of his wound, Hunt scooped her up in his arms, carried her from the bathroom to his bed, and gently seated her on the edge. "I've been fighting my desires from the moment I first saw you at the Swanson's party. If you tell me no, I'll respect your wishes. I don't want you to feel like you're trapped at my house without any options. But if you want this stopped, you'd better say so right now."

He hadn't realized he'd been holding his breath until he expelled it in a sigh of relief when she answered him by winding her arms around his neck. No more holding back. This woman who had captured his full attention, who had constantly been in his thoughts, a woman different from any he had known, would be spending the night in his bed.

He reached for her shirt, but she stopped him. A hint

of disappointment intruded into the moment. Had he so totally misinterpreted her actions? Had he allowed his desires to overrule reality?

"I can do that quicker than you can." Her soft words drifted over him, cloaked in the huskiness of arousal.

Clothes quickly fell away. Bare skin clung to bare skin along the length of their bodies. Sexual electricity crackled through the air. He danced his fingers across the swell of her breast before cupping it in his palm. The creamy texture of her skin fueled his already fully extended arousal. Everything about her excited his senses. He drew her puckered nipple into his mouth, teased it with his tongue, then sucked.

Aurora arched her hips upward, inviting his attention at the same time as she skimmed her hands across his muscled back and down to his rear end. He answered her need by tickling his fingers up her inner thigh until he reached her feminine folds. Inserting a finger, he stimulated her. Just his touch excited her more than she had imagined. It had been a long, busy, and exhausting day, but sleep was the farthest thing from her mind.

His touch was like no other. Waves of delight washed over her. Never had she been propelled so quickly or easily toward the ultimate ecstasy. He again captured her mouth with a heated kiss. She rapidly lost herself totally and completely to the passion that personified Huntington Wolfe III. The contractions began deep inside her and radiated through her body. Her heart pounded and her pulse raced. Her mind swirled in a fog of euphoria.

Hunt didn't know how much longer he could hold off. His desire for her had continued to simmer just below the surface from the moment of their first kiss after they went sailing. He had never wanted a woman as much as he wanted Aurora Brentano. Had the danger earlier that evening heightened his already intense desires?

Maybe so, but that did not diminish the much deeper longing he felt toward her. Something on an entirely different plane of existence, something much more than physical needs or desire for a beautiful woman. The growing awareness was decidedly personal, and he couldn't deny it was laden with a heavy dose of emotion.

Reaching for the nightstand, he pulled open the drawer, grabbed a condom, and sheathed his erection. He slowly penetrated the moist heat of her body, the enormity of the moment nearly taking his breath away. They moved together in perfect harmony as if they were long time lovers, each able to fully anticipate what pleased the other—a night of making love that felt as if it would last forever.

Chapter Seven

Aurora stretched, turned onto her back, and opened her eyes. She slowly looked around, taking in all the details of Hunt's bedroom. It hadn't been a dream. The most incredible night of her life had really happened. She wrinkled her brow into a slight frown as she stared at the empty space next to her, still showing the impression of where his body had been. She touched the sheets but didn't detect any lingering body heat. He obviously had been up for a while.

Her feeling of blissful contentment quickly faded away, replaced by a troubling confusion. Where had he gone? Why had he left her alone? Was it his way of maintaining a distance between them? Making sure she understood that it was just sex and nothing more? No emotional attachment? No strings?

Then her gaze fell on her suitcase. He had brought it from the downstairs guest room. A hopeful spark ignited deep inside her. Was it his way of saying he wanted her to stay in his room rather than the guest room for the duration of her time in his house? Or was he simply making sure she had something to put on when she got up in order to prevent the intimacy of her using his robe? Or an even more disturbing possibility, was it his way of letting her know it was time for her to leave?

The spark quickly died. Waking up alone wasn't how she had anticipated the *morning after*.

But in the clear light of day, did she have regrets? No...absolutely not.

She slid out of bed, took some clothes from her suitcase, and went to his bathroom. She emerged twenty minutes later, showered and dressed. As soon as she opened the bathroom door, the aroma of freshly brewed coffee greeted her.

"Good morning," Hunt called to her from the sitting room. He had set out breakfast on the bistro table—a filled coffee carafe on a warming pad, freshly sliced honeydew melon, and warm croissants.

"You fixed breakfast?" She was having trouble pulling all the pieces together. He brought up her suitcase, then prepared breakfast, and brought it upstairs. Definitely not the actions of a man trying to tell a woman it hadn't been anything more than a one-night stand.

"I don't know if you normally eat a full breakfast or not, so I decided to go with the basic continental breakfast. If you want something more, I can whip up some scrambled eggs and bacon."

"No, this is great. Thank you." She locked gazes with him, holding it for a heated moment. "You shouldn't have gone to all this trouble."

"It wasn't any trouble. I wanted to do it." He held out his hand and pulled her into his arms, placing a tender kiss on her forehead. "Did you sleep well?"

Embarrassment tugged at her, causing her to glance out the window at the lake. "I've never slept better. How about you?"

His features turned serious as he brushed another kiss against her lips. "Falling asleep with a beautiful woman in my arms...what more could a man want?"

She didn't have a clue how to respond to what he

had said. But a deeper fear was that she might have misinterpreted his meaning, that of sharing a night of incredible sex. Or was he talking specifically about her? Did she dare hope?

They ate breakfast, neither mentioning what had happened between them. It was almost as if talking about it would somehow lessen the emotional impact of a special night.

"Hey…Hunt? Are you awake?" Johnny yelled from downstairs rather than coming through the intercom.

Hunt walked over to the door and called down to Johnny, "What's up?"

"Turn on the news."

Hunt grabbed the remote and clicked on the television in the sitting room.

"…are making this a priority matter. To repeat, our top story of the morning—Detective Roger Whitcomb of the Seattle Police Department was found dead in his car shortly after midnight by a police officer on routine patrol in Discovery Park. The police haven't released any further details, but sources say this is being treated as a murder investigation. There is speculation that Detective Whitcomb's death is tied to the spectacular jewel thefts that have plagued the area for the last five years, the most recent one a week ago. A highly placed source said they believe Quentin Brentano, their primary suspect, had an accomplice who is now acting on his or her own. Brentano's daughter, Aurora, has been mentioned as a person of interest in this continuing investigation. The authorities are trying to locate her. She has been living in San Francisco. Quentin Brentano perished almost three months ago in a fiery crash following a high-speed chase with the Seattle police."

The stunned look on Hunt's face matched the shock Aurora felt. "Dead?" Confusion surrounded her words. "Johnny said he saw Roger last night at the time we were leaving to meet with him. So he must have died later than that…but how? He was still in the park, so he must have been killed before the appointed time we were to meet him, otherwise he wouldn't have been there."

Hunt shook his head as a frown wrinkled across his forehead. "No, that isn't what Johnny said. He saw *someone* sitting behind the wheel of Roger's car. It could have been Roger alive, or it could just as easily have been someone else. Or it could have been Roger already dead."

"And now they're looking for me?" A quick jolt of panic hit her. This couldn't be happening. She felt as if she had lost all control of her own life. "Why would they think I had anything to do with the thefts? And, surely, they can't believe I have some connection to my father's death."

They hurried downstairs and found Johnny in the kitchen drinking coffee and watching the news.

Hunt sat next to him. "What happened in the park last night?"

Johnny shook his head as if trying to call up a memory that wasn't really there. "That's just it. Nothing happened. I had just arrived, did a quick reconnaissance of the area, spotted his car in the parking lot with someone sitting behind the wheel. There wasn't anyone else in sight or any other cars. That's when Aurora called. I immediately headed back here. That's it."

A scowl spread across Hunt's face. "I wonder if there were any signs of robbery, a man sitting alone in his car in a deserted parking lot."

Johnny shook his head. "The news story didn't mention it, and I didn't go near his car."

"Either this has something to do with the reason Roger wanted to meet with me, or it's an incredible coincidence that someone would kill him at the time and place where he was waiting for us to arrive." He stared at Johnny, then Aurora, then Johnny again. "And I don't believe in spectacular coincidences. That leaves us with the unanswered questions of what Roger wanted with us, who would be threatened by it, and why?"

Johnny nodded his head in agreement. "And it's obviously somehow tied in with someone taking a shot at you."

"Yes…again a coincidence that I'm not buying. Maybe it was someone's way of keeping us occupied so we wouldn't make contact with Roger, not even by cell phone." Hunt thought for a moment. "Is there any way you can computer enhance the front gate security video from last night? Anything you can do to make the mysterious figure who hid behind the trash barrels clearer? Or pick up any identifying features on the car?"

Johnny shook his head. "I've already tried. There's nothing that would help. Whoever it was had purposely covered both the front and rear license plate on the car. And as far as a recognizable face…between a turned-up collar on his jacket, a hat, and keeping his head down, there wasn't any of his face to enhance. Whoever it was either knew about the camera or is experienced in skulking around and automatically assumed there would be cameras in place since most of the houses in this area have extensive security systems. In fact, we were one of the last of the residents to expand our security system to include all the grounds."

Hunt stared at the floor for several seconds, then grabbed the phone and quickly hit a speed dial number.

"Rita...what's the information on Roger Whitcomb? The news this morning said *sources* were treating it as a murder investigation. What do you know that's not being released to the media?"

"This is real touchy, Hunt. The murder of a police officer is extremely high priority, and this one has all the earmarks of a setup. Roger wasn't officially on duty and hadn't mentioned anything to anyone about a meet, but there's no other reason for him to be in that area at that time of night just sitting all alone in his car in the dark."

"How was he killed? Any word from the coroner? What about time of death?"

"There is no official word yet, but unofficially, it was a small caliber shot to the left temple at close range. As far as I know, they haven't pinpointed a time of death yet."

"So it would have been someone standing next to the car door on the driver's side. Any shattered glass?"

"No, the window was down." Rita paused as if trying to find the proper words. "And his weapon was still holstered with the flap snapped shut. You know as well as I do what that means."

"He knew the shooter and wasn't concerned." His words were almost a whisper, more along the lines of thinking out loud. "And what's this I heard on the news about Brentano's daughter now being a *person of interest*? Who's brilliant idea was that...as if I didn't know."

Rita's laugh told him she knew exactly what he was talking about. "Yeah, the ever popular and always charming Lt. Montrose pulled that little tidbit out of thin air and added it to the mix early this morning." Then her voice turned serious. "Why all this interest? What's going on?"

"Last night someone took a shot at me. Seems to have been a night for people running around shooting at people."

"Someone shot at you?" No mistaking Rita's shock and deep concern. "Are you okay?"

"Just a minor flesh wound, no big deal. Didn't even need stitches. The other two shots slammed into the wall by the front door."

"Three shots? Someone took three shots at you? Why would someone want to shoot you? Do you have any idea who it was?"

"Don't worry about it. Probably just a drive-by."

"In Medina?"

"Yeah, well…" Hunt quickly changed the subject. "I know you're busy, so I'll let you get back to work. Thanks for the info. Give me a call as soon as the coroner fixes the time of death."

He disconnected from the call and quickly relayed the conversation to Johnny and Aurora. She immediately said what was on everyone's mind. "Could Roger have been surprised by someone he mistook for you in the dark?"

"I don't know, but it sure seems logical. In the dark he could have assumed it was me and rolled down the window."

Johnny interrupted Hunt's train of thought. "No, I don't think so. He'd been a cop too long to be caught like that. Roger and you aren't exactly friends. Even if he thought it was you approaching his car, he would have been on the alert even though he was the one who requested the meet. He would have had his weapon at the ready just in case."

Aurora added her thoughts. "Maybe he had some information about my father? I don't know why else he would have wanted me to be there, too. But what would have warranted a secret meeting?"

Hunt reached out and took her hand. "He might have uncovered information he wanted to sell you, something incriminating, and he was trying to make a profit. After all, Montrose has named you a person of interest."

"If Roger knew my true identity, doesn't that mean Lt. Montrose does, too?"

"Not necessarily." Hunt's forehead wrinkled into a slight frown. "If Roger did know, he might have kept it to himself. I've noticed a couple of times Montrose said or did something in his usual offensive manner that elicited a disapproving look from Roger." He turned toward Johnny. "I think it might be prudent for Aurora and me to get out of town for a couple of days before someone figures out they can find her here."

"You mean leave the country?"

"No. I mean stay close by, but not here. Even though my house is secure—" A soft chuckle containing a hint of irony escaped his throat. "—except for someone shooting at us from the street, of course. We need a place to go where we won't have to constantly be looking over our shoulders. And I don't think we should be here in case someone comes looking for us.

"I want to know about any inquiry, no matter how innocent or inconsequential. Anything…someone buzzing from the front gate claiming to be taking a survey. The police, especially if they're from the jewel theft task force that Montrose heads. Anyone from the

DA's office. Anyone asking, you don't know anything about Gwen really being Aurora and you don't know where either one of us went. If they get pushy, demanding an answer, tell them you're not my keeper. You're only the guy who stays in the guest house sometimes. Since I'm gone so much, you're the official house sitter. Anything that looks like it's about to escalate, call the police.

"If someone shows up with a search warrant, call Frank Tanner and the police. The Medina police will make sure that Montrose and his task force members don't exceed the parameters of that warrant and that it's properly served."

Johnny allowed a chuckle. "Keep Montrose in line? I can do that. No problem."

Hunt paused a moment as he put a new thought together. "Just to further confuse the issue, should someone come looking for either me or Aurora, drive us to the Yacht Club so there will be a record of us leaving on my boat. You can say the last time you saw either of us was when you dropped us off at the Yacht Club. Then we'll meet you at Pirate's Cove. We'll take the car, and you dock the boat somewhere off the beaten path for the time being. Take it out to the San Juan Islands and dock it at Friday Harbor or Orcas Island if you have to. Will you be able to get back home without a problem?"

"Easy. I can take the commuter flight from Friday Harbor to Seattle."

"If anyone comes asking, let me know right away. Make sure to use the disposables."

"Do you have someplace in mind?"

Aurora quickly spoke up. "I know the perfect place."

"Then let's do it before someone tells me not to leave town"—he glanced at Aurora—"or shows up looking for Quentin Brentano's daughter. Between Roger insisting that you come with me and Montrose being face-to-face with you twice in one day, I think it's a good bet that someone knows your true identity—the name you're using and where to find you."

Aurora grabbed her suitcase from upstairs, and Hunt threw some clothes in a weekend bag. In fifteen minutes, they left through the front gate. Johnny drove them in Hunt's SUV, visible to anyone watching. They went straight to the Yacht Club.

****

It was late afternoon when Hunt pulled Johnny's surveillance car behind the mountain cabin on Washington's Olympic Peninsula so that it was hidden from view. He had taken cash from his safe to prevent a digital trail. He had also taken the 9mm and 25 caliber handguns. They had brought supplies with them to last for a couple of days so they wouldn't need to stop along the way.

Aurora unlocked the cabin door. She looked around, taking in everything she remembered from years ago before she moved to San Francisco. "Like I said, no luxuries, but that also means no utilities for someone to trace. The deed to the property and the taxes are in my mother's maiden name. She inherited it from her parents, and my father never changed anything over. No way anyone can find us here. No television, but you can get a couple of radio stations. Surprisingly, there is cell phone reception unless there's a storm. There's nothing here that relates to me or can be connected to the name Brentano. It's a perfect hiding place...as long as you don't mind cold water and an outhouse."

Hunt quickly surveyed the premises, checking doors and windows to make sure everything was secure. The main room consisted of a combination living area with sofa bed, dining table, and small kitchenette with two burner propane stove and propane refrigerator. An alcove off to one side with a curtain separating it from the main room was just large enough to hold a double bed and dresser. The only running water came from a hand pump at the kitchen sink that pulled water from a well. A wood burning fireplace provided the only heat. An outhouse was located behind the cabin and a side porch had a makeshift shower with solar heat for the cold well water. Definitely basic and off the grid.

While he checked the kerosene lanterns to verify they were functional, she went to put away the supplies. The first thing to do was turn on the propane refrigerator. She opened the refrigerator door and instantly froze on the spot. A hard jolt of panic hit her along with a huge dose of trepidation. Her mouth went dry accompanied by the pounding of her heart. She tried to swallow the lump in her throat without any success.

She finally managed to force out some shaky words, the quaver in her voice clearly evident. "Someone's been here."

Hunt turned, seeking out what had grabbed her attention. Then he saw it. The refrigerator had been turned on and contained food. "I thought you said nobody knew about this place."

"No one does." She picked up a couple of items from the refrigerator and checked the expiration dates. "This is fresh. Someone has been here in the last couple of days."

He saw the fear in her eyes and immediately went to her. Pulling her into his embrace, he held her close. Her pounding heart reverberated to him. From the moment he first saw her, he had noticed how she carried herself with confidence. Someone who knew who she was, where she was going, and how to get there. Someone who could think for herself—brains and good instincts. The independent woman he found so appealing. But in spite of the brave front she tried to project, he could tell she was frightened. And understandably so.

Hunt pulled her into his embrace. "Try not to worry." He brushed her hair from her cheek. "Everything's going to be okay. It's probably just some transient who realized the cabin was not being used and decided to move in for a while."

Those may have been his words, but whatever was going on had just taken a sharp turn into weird, or more accurately, weirder. The cabin was too far off the beaten path for someone to accidently stumble upon it. The closest source for food was a mile away via a dirt road to the two-lane paved road where the general store was located that served the area. And there hadn't been any signs of someone breaking in—no broken windows and the doors didn't appear to have been forced.

"Is there anything here that seems out of place? Something that doesn't belong to you or your father?"

"I didn't notice when we walked in, but I wasn't looking for anything suspicious. I'll take a closer look, but it's been a few years since I was here."

He studied her as she inspected the cabin, including the sleeping alcove. Feelings he didn't want to deal with forced themselves into the open. Everything about her. More than just good looks and a heated passion that nearly knocked his socks off. The total package. Beauty and brains—and so much more. He tried to remind himself of his obligation to Excellence Insurance and his investigation, but his concern for Aurora's safety shoved everything else aside.

"Nothing else seems to be out of place. There's some of my father's clothes, but he always kept extra clothes here. I…I don't know what to make of the fresh food." She attempted to project a confident image, but he saw right through it. "I'm sure there's nothing to it. Nothing to worry about."

He flashed a smile. "I'm sure you're right."

Hunt built a small fire in the fireplace, just enough to take the chill out of the air but not large enough to burn for long. They settled on the couch. He put his arm around her and pulled her close. "Someone taking a shot at us has to connect to the jewel thefts and your father's death. And it has to somehow tie in with Whitcomb's murder. Otherwise, there's just too many unrelated coincidences to be viable. Too many odd things all happening at the same time. Everything's somehow connected. We just need to figure out which puzzle pieces fit, where they fit, dismiss the ones that don't belong, then determine the total picture."

He allowed a thoughtful expression as he ran through the events of the last few days. "Someone was watching my house the day we went sailing, which means one of two things. Either someone was following you, or I was under suspicion, even though I had an airtight alibi of being out of the country on three of the dates when jewelry was stolen. Checking out Charlie Gorman's little black book revealed his bookie operation, which accounts for his suspicious activity and unexplained income. That moves him down the list but doesn't eliminate Charlie as a suspect.

"Then there's your feeling of being watched, and someone waiting for you at your father's house, then taking off when he realized you weren't alone, which says someone knew your real identity. Roger Whitcomb's call wanting to meet with both of us for some unknown reason makes me wonder if Roger wanted you there because he knew who you are. Then someone shot at us as we left to meet Roger. And finally, Roger's murder." He slowly shook his head. "It's all connected. Somehow, all those loose pieces fit together to form a cohesive picture...but a picture of what? I feel like it's right there, but I can't quite put my finger on it."

Aurora suddenly sat upright. "Stu Allen."

"What about him?"

"We checked on Charlie, but not on Stu. Johnny looked into his trips out of state to visit a sick mother, which didn't show anything more than that. He doesn't have a little black book like Charlie and doesn't live on his cell phone, but we didn't check any further than those trips. As we thought earlier, Prestige Caterers is in a perfect position to be involved in the thefts." She bit at her lower lip. "I need to get back to the catering offices again. This time, I'll take a look inside Stu's wallet."

"But there's nothing to connect Prestige with the shooting at my house or the murder of Roger Whitcomb."

"Just because we don't know of a connection doesn't mean there isn't one. I think I should hit the offices tomorrow. Charlie comes in early to work before anyone else comes in. Stu doesn't come in until late morning. If I stop by to check on the schedule about noon, Charlie will be out to lunch and Stu will be in the kitchen."

"Charlie doesn't eat in?"

"Rarely, from what I hear. I always thought that was odd, especially since Stu is a top-notch chef and could easily put something together for lunch."

"I can't allow you to—"

Her body stiffened as she pulled away from him. "You can't *allow* me? You're *telling* me what to do?" Her anger flared. "One night in bed doesn't give you the right to tell me what I can and can't do."

"Rein in that indignation and let me finish what I was saying." He wasn't sure how to respond to her outburst, especially the comment about spending the night making love. "First…I would never try to take away your right to make your own decisions. One of the many things I find so appealing about you is your independence."

"I…" A pink tinge of embarrassment spread across her cheeks. "I guess my nerves are a little bit on edge. I didn't mean to snap at you."

"No harm done. What I was about to say is that I can't allow you to go alone. I'm going with you. This isn't like Charlie's book where you were able to grab it from his desk, then pretend it fell on the floor with a stack of papers. Stu keeps his wallet on his person. Maybe you can accidently bump into him once to lift it and take it out of the room to search it. But bumping into him twice so you can return it? That's too risky. I'll keep Stu busy by telling him I'm planning a party and want to discuss the menu. I'll provide the distraction while you handle the wallet."

"I sure wish we had that handy little scanning thing

of Johnny's. That worked real well."

"True, but there shouldn't be that much information in Stu's wallet. Just use the camera on your phone."

Aurora leaned back and gave him an appraising look. A rush of anxiety hit him. He tried to carefully pick his words, not at all sure where this sudden turn of events was headed. "What's the matter? What's that look all about?"

"You seem to be very good at all this detective type stuff…almost as if you've had a lot of experience." She glanced down, then back up, determination etching her features. "What is there you aren't telling me? You perpetuate the persona of a rich playboy living on the family money. Someone shallow and self-serving. Yet there's a highly intelligent person with a clear cut sense of responsibility lurking behind that façade. Why do you choose to hide that person away? Why do you want people to think of you as so much less than you are?"

Hunt sucked in a steadying breath. "Wow…I didn't see that one coming." How much to tell her. If he was going to pursue a relationship with her, he knew this moment would eventually present itself. He just hadn't been prepared for it being quite so soon. It all came down to whether he trusted her…trusted her implicitly. He thought of the previous night when they had made love. He took another deep breath, then made his decision.

"You're right. There's more going on here than you know. Contrary to popular opinion and ongoing gossip, I'm totally self-supporting and am not squandering the family fortune on wine, women, and song. I have a bachelor's degree in business administration and a master's degree in finance. I head up all the family business interests, but I don't micro-manage, nor do I take a salary. I hire capable people who know their jobs and let them do what they were hired to do. We have management meetings once a month, and I'm available by phone at all times should problems arise, but I don't maintain an office presence.

"As far as this *detective type stuff*, as you put it, I do know quite a bit about it. I work as a freelance investigator for a select few clients, the primary one being Excellence Insurance. I'm currently contracted to locate the pieces of stolen jewelry insured by them. Between what my investigations pay me and my earnings on investments, they comfortably support my somewhat lavish lifestyle."

"I see." She got up and walked over to the fireplace. She held out her hands toward the flames in an attempt to warm the sudden chill that invaded her body. "Your offer to help me find the truth about my father's death was only a cover for your investigation. You believe my father is guilty, so I must know something about what he did with the stolen property. You stick with me, get me to trust you, and hope I'll lead you to what you want." The look of disappointment on her face was nothing compared to the hurt in her voice.

And it tore through him with a pain unlike anything he had previously experienced. An emotional pain he couldn't explain and didn't totally understand.

He walked over to the fireplace and pulled her into his arms. She didn't resist, but she didn't respond, either. At that moment, nothing else mattered except repairing the sudden rift between them. It was time for complete honesty.

"I can't explain everything that's happened—"

"I understand the need to maintain confidentiality

with your client." Her words came out flat, her voice without emotion.

"Hold on—once again you're jumping to conclusions. You're *understanding me* too quickly. I didn't say I *won't* explain, I said I *can't*. I don't know how all these pieces fit together…at least not yet. But I can assure you of one thing. I'm not stringing you along in an attempt to get information from you. I honestly and sincerely want to help you find the truth about your father's death. I've already had two emails and a phone call from Excellence Insurance's CEO in London about my lack of progress reports on their case. I chose to put them off and pursue the case from the perspective of your father rather than concentrating solely on the stolen jewelry.

"From the moment I was handed this investigation and started going through the background information, I found the circumstances surrounding your father's death suspicious. When I found out it was Montrose who was chasing him when his car went off the cliff, that sent up a whole bunch of red flags for me. Johnny and I are a close-knit team for a specific reason. We have worked together for a long time. I trust him implicitly. I haven't been stringing you along to get your trust. In fact, the personal information I just shared with you about my life and my job was me giving you *my* trust."

Hunt's words penetrated Aurora's hurt and despair. He was right. He had just trusted her with highly confidential information. And there was his other comment…Montrose again. "You mentioned that you had a history with the lieutenant. I know why I don't like him, but what's your relationship to him? Why do you convey such contempt whenever his name is mentioned?"

A hint of a bittersweet chuckle escaped his throat. "You're going to end up prying the complete story of my entire life out of me if I'm not careful."

"Only what you want to tell me. I'd rather you didn't say anything than to have you lie to me…again." She had been angry and hurt at first. Now, she was mostly confused. She didn't know how much of what he had told her to believe. Or for that matter, whether she should believe anything he had said. She wanted to believe him, but she wasn't sure.

He tightened his hold on her. She wanted to resist his touch, to break free of his embrace. Instead, she found herself slipping her arms around his waist. He caressed her shoulders and back. There was something so comforting about his touch. In spite of what he had revealed, she still felt safe with him. She didn't understand it, but she couldn't deny it.

"Montrose and I have a long, adversarial history. I was quite serious in what I told you about the reputation of my attorney and my family name and money being the only thing that has kept him from going too far in his pursuit of me. Had it not been for that, I'm sure he would have tried to frame me a long time ago."

"Frame you for what? Why are you such a major sore spot with him?"

"It has to do with a string of jewel thefts several years ago, some of which occurred in this area. He had it in his head that I was the master cat burglar—much in the same way as he focused on your father—and was frustrated because he couldn't prove it. He had taken me in for questioning any number of times but never found any evidence to justify an arrest. So, naturally, when this recent string of thefts started five years ago, he immediately looked to me. The fact that I could prove I wasn't even in the country when three of the thefts occurred hasn't deterred him in his overzealous pursuit. Even though I don't live in Seattle, as the head of a multi-jurisdictional task force that includes the cooperation of the Medina police, he feels it gives him legal right to show up at my house whenever he wants without the necessity of a legal leg to stand on."

"Such as last night," she said. "Even though the matter was a local one, the Medina police already on the scene, and didn't involve stolen jewels?"

"Exactly." He cocked his head and shot her a questioning look. "Any more questions you'd like me to answer?"

"No. I understand why you would have been suspicious of me, especially with me taking a job under an assumed name and then me lifting that wallet. I don't have any more questions. I hope your concerns about me have been resolved."

Everything he had just told her was quite a surprise and certainly explained a lot while answering several unasked questions. She wanted to ask *the* question, to ask if he was that master jewel thief from several years ago. To ask if he was involved in the current thefts.

But she couldn't ask. She either trusted him or she didn't. He had demonstrated his trust in her. And the bottom line…she believed what he had told her. Regardless of any unanswered questions, she trusted him.

They remained wrapped in each other's arms, neither saying anything as they shared a moment of deep emotional bonding. A moment abruptly broken by the ringing of Hunt's disposable cell phone.

"What's up, Johnny?"

"A couple of things. First, the black car with the dark tinted windows is back. Whoever is in it drove by slowly a couple of times but didn't stop. The surveillance footage didn't reveal anything new. No visual on the driver, and both license plates on the car are still obscured with mud. The one difference is that, this time, the entire car is dirty. It looked like it had been traveling on dirt roads."

"And second?"

"Medina police were here claiming it was just a routine follow up. They asked about your arm."

"That's not so unusual." An amused chuckle escaped his throat. "I think it's just a matter of keeping us *high profile* residents happy." He paused a moment. "That's probably an unfair statement. They're conscientious about their job and taking care of the community they serve."

"Yeah, but it doesn't explain why Montrose was tagging along with them."

"Montrose?" Hunt tightened his jaw at the mention of his nemesis' name. "What was it this time, another of his *just in the neighborhood* excuses?"

"He apparently felt he didn't need to give me an explanation. After pointing out that your SUV was parked in the drive, he asked where your Porsche was. I told him it was in the garage, and he told me to open the garage door so he could verify it. I *suggested* he get a warrant, then told him to get off the property. I thanked the Medina police for their consideration and assured them I'd let you know they had stopped by to see how you were doing. Montrose started to take exception to me ordering him off property I didn't own. I told him to take it up with Frank Tanner. That kind of put an end to the conversation. The Medina police politely but emphatically moved Montrose toward the entrance gates while shooting me one of those looks that said they don't have any use for him, either."

"Did Montrose arrive with the police, or was he in his own car?"

"He was in his own car. He walked in the gate when I opened it to admit the police car."

"Did he say anything about Roger's murder? Make mention of the coincidence of it happening on the same night that someone took a shot at us?"

"Not a word."

"Montrose has crossed the line coming to my house and demanding information without cause. I'll give Frank a call and let him know Montrose is harassing me again. He can casually mention it to Seattle's Chief of Police tomorrow at their regular weekly golf game."

"Maybe…" Johnny paused as if trying to gather his words. "Maybe it would be better if I did it. After all, I was the one he confronted while you were allegedly out of town. You don't need a record of an incoming call to your attorney's office from an untraceable number and have someone wonder why you have it, and you certainly don't want to turn on your cell, in case someone is waiting for a signal to ping a tower."

"Good thought." They talked for another minute before ending the call. Hunt relayed the conversation to Aurora. "So we have the mysterious black car again."

Aurora glanced at her watch. "It's getting late. We should probably fix something to eat then decide on a plan of action for checking out Stu Allen."

****

Hunt didn't know exactly what woke him. It was too dark to see anything. He remained still and listened. He had almost decided it had been his imagination, perhaps a bit of a dream or an animal outside on the prowl, then he heard the cabin door open and someone enter. A jolt of adrenaline surged through his veins as he snapped to attention. It had been the sound of a car arriving—the engine and the car door—that woke him.

A flashlight beam moved across the main room and came to rest on one of the lanterns. Then he made out the shadowy form of a man, medium height, who seemed to be searching for something. Had Montrose somehow managed to track him? Was he after Aurora? After both of them?

Aurora stirred. Hunt immediately quieted her, whispered in her ear, then grabbed his 9mm from the floor next to the bed. His heartbeat jumped into high gear as he made his way silently across the room from the sleeping alcove and came up behind the intruder. A moment later, he tackled the stranger.

The two men grappled on the floor, knocking over a small table and breaking a glass. Hunt took a hit to the jaw before managing to secure his arm across the man's neck in a choke hold. As soon as he pressed the muzzle of the gun against the intruder's temple, the man instantly stopped struggling.

"Don't shoot. I'm not armed."

Hunt called to Aurora, "Let's get some light over here."

She moved quickly to follow his directions. Clicking on the flashlight, she shined it on the man. A startled gasp escaped her throat as she staggered backward a couple of steps.

"Daddy?" The single word came out as a strained whisper, her voice filled with shock and disbelief.

Hunt turned loose and spun the man around so he could see the intruder's face. A face he instantly recognized, one he had studied in several photographs and newspaper clippings.

Quentin Brentano in person...alive and apparently well.

Chapter Eight

"I don't understand," Aurora stared at her father. "How could you do this to me? It's been almost three months since the car crash. Why did you let me believe you were dead? Why didn't you let me know you were alive?"

Hunt watched and listened. Emotional turmoil ravaged her face and filled her voice. His first instinct had been to jump in and take charge, find out everything Quentin knew, but he held back. She deserved answers first. Then he would get the information he needed.

"I'm sorry, Rora." Quentin's voice carried unmistakably deep emotion.

Moisture filled her eyes when he used what was obviously a pet name for his daughter.

Quentin placed his hands gently on her shoulders. "It never occurred to me that you'd come to Seattle and start your own investigation. But once you got here, I knew the only way to protect you was to make sure I didn't have any contact with you, not even a phone call. I couldn't take a chance that someone would come after you."

"Protect me from what?"

Quentin took a deep breath and slowly shook his head. "That's just it. I don't know."

"But why were the police chasing you? What happened? How did you escape?"

Quentin threw a contemptuous glance in Hunt's direction, then returned his attention to his daughter. "How did you get hooked up with this guy?"

"Well—"

"*This guy* has a name." Hunt stepped forward to confront Quentin. Fixing him with a hard stare, Hunt took command of the situation. "It's Huntington Wolfe III. My *friends* call me Hunt, but you can address me as Mr. Wolfe. I first encountered your daughter at the Swanson's party where I was a guest and she was working for the catering company under a false identity. I watched as she deftly picked a man's pocket and walked off with his wallet. Before I could decide how to handle the situation, I saw her return the wallet intact.

"Later that night, the Swansons became the most recent victims in the string of jewelry thefts. Needless to say, that captured my attention and curiosity. I made it a point of tracking her down. I learned her real name when I traced the car she was driving, the one with the California license plates. And that was how she *hooked up with this guy*. Now, I'm anxious to hear your answers to her questions."

Hunt caught the look Aurora threw his way. He leaned back and let her take over. Hopefully, that would produce the information he needed with a minimum of conflict.

"Tell me what happened, daddy. How did you get into this mess?"

"Beyond maybe being in the wrong place at the wrong time, I honestly don't know. I intellectually understand why the police would consider me a suspect. I'm an expert on gems. I possess sleight of hand skills, which certainly doesn't extend to overriding security systems or opening safes. I performed my magic act at several of the parties where the thefts occurred. I found out that being home alone, asleep in my own bed, isn't much of an alibi. Every time I turned around, I found myself staring at Lt. Montrose. And at other times, I knew I was being followed. They weren't even subtle about it. The situation had turned from suspicion to all out harassment. I even consulted an attorney, but it didn't get me anywhere."

"Why didn't you tell me what was going on?" Aurora's eyes pleaded for answers. "I could have helped you."

"The last thing I wanted to do was put you in danger. No one believed I was being harassed by the police, in particular by Lt. Montrose."

"Well, Quentin, this is your lucky day." Hunt sat in a chair facing Aurora and her father who both sat on the sofa. "You have stumbled across the one person who absolutely knows from experience that Lt. Montrose routinely abuses his power and harasses people without cause other than his own personal agenda, arrogance, and ego. He's more than capable of setting up someone if he thinks it would get him what he wanted."

Quentin addressed his question directly to Hunt. "But what would he want with me?"

"He has a high-profile case, and he needs it solved. You have all the credentials to be the perfect fall guy which gives him another fifteen minutes of fame."

"But what would he gain by that? He arrests me, but as soon as another theft occurs, it's obvious I'm not their man."

"Which is exactly what happened. Everyone thought you were dead, yet the thefts started up again.

Montrose immediately claimed you had an accomplice who had never been previously mentioned. This alleged accomplice continued after your death. It probably frustrated him big time when your car went over that cliff and your body was never recovered."

Aurora covered her father's hand. "How did you manage to survive that awful car crash?"

A slight grin tugged at the corners of Quentin Brentano's mouth. "My magician's skills may not include the ability to disarm a security system or crack a safe, but they do allow me to stage an illusion or two. I believe the car crash was one of my best. I rigged the car to explode by remote control. I led the lieutenant on a chase along a well-planned route with a pre-determined spot where they would lose sight of me for a few seconds around a curve in the road. I bailed out of the moving car before they caught up to me again. I rolled into some brush and hit the remote as the car reached the rocks at the bottom of the cliff making it appear to explode on impact. I managed to get away in the darkness and confusion while everyone's attention was focused on the crash. I picked up my motorcycle from where I had hidden it and disappeared into the night."

Hunt shook his head. "That was an incredibly risky move. You could have been severely injured jumping out of a fast-moving vehicle."

"Yes, daddy. You could have been killed."

He patted her hand in a fatherly manner. "I didn't have any choice, Rora. I had a sincere belief that the lieutenant was about to arrest me and would do whatever he needed to do to make it stick, including lying and planting evidence." A thoughtful look crossed his face. "Possibly even arranging for me to have some sort of an *accident,* one in which I didn't have control of the outcome."

"Have you been hiding out here at the cabin all this time?" Lines of tension continued to etch her face even though her body language had relaxed a little bit.

"Yes, for the most part."

Hunt eyed him suspiciously. "I heard a car pull up and a door close, not a motorcycle. That's what woke me."

Aurora sat upright and stared at her father. "Your motorcycle is parked in the garage at your house."

"I know. I spent two weeks working out all the details of my disappearance and that included procuring a car that couldn't be traced to me and making sure I had as much cash as I could get my hands on so I wouldn't leave a paper trail."

"So tell us, Quentin, how have you been spending your time since your untimely death?"

Quentin stared at Hunt for a moment, as if considering several possibilities before responding. "Well, since my daughter's arrival, I've been doing my best to keep a watchful eye on her. I was decidedly unhappy when I followed her to that house in Medina, especially after I discovered who lives there."

Hunt jerked to attention. "You've been watching my house? Did you pick up on anyone else watching it?"

"I haven't really been watching your house, certainly not on a regular basis. I've been watching my daughter."

"You're the one driving the black car with the dark tinted windows and the mud splattered on the license plates? You were parked across from my driveway the afternoon Aurora and I went sailing?"

"Yes, that was me."

She reached for Quentin's hand. "I've had such a creepy feeling that someone was watching me, but I never saw anyone. It really had my nerves on end. It's such a relief to find out it was you."

"I certainly didn't mean to frighten you. I tried to let you know I was alive. I approached you last night at my house—"

She gasped. "That was you? You scared the hell out of me!"

"I'm sorry." Quentin squeezed her hand. "I've been in such turmoil from the moment I realized you had come back to Seattle and were staying at my house. I knew I had to keep my distance from you. I was sure Lt. Montrose would put you under surveillance if he knew you were here. But instead of being able to communicate with you, I apparently only succeeded in driving you to his...uh, to *Mr. Wolfe's* house."

Despair and helplessness flashed across Quentin's face, and it tugged at Hunt's emotions. "You can call me Hunt." It was blatantly obvious how much he loved his daughter and his genuine concern for her safety. "Last night, Quentin—were you watching my house when someone took a shot at us?"

His eyes grew wide in shock as he sat in stunned silence for a moment. "Someone took a shot at you?" He grabbed his daughter. "Are you okay? Were you hurt?"

"I'm fine," she assured her father. "It was Hunt who was hurt. A bullet grazed his arm. I wasn't injured, just very frightened."

Quentin shot a disdainful look at Hunt. "Then you were the target, not my daughter? She's in danger because of you?"

Aurora put her hand on Quentin's arm in an attempt to calm him. "No, daddy. That's not the way it is."

Hunt leveled a steady gaze at Quentin. "Well, can I take that to mean you were not watching my house last night and can't provide any information about who might have taken a shot at us?"

Quentin paused, as if trying to decide what to do. Then his body language relaxed a little and he leaned back. "I drove by your house, but before I could decide what to do, I saw Lt. Montrose. I kept on going. I couldn't take a chance on sticking around and having him spot me."

Hunt nodded in agreement. "Probably the wisest thing to do."

They continued to talk for another two hours, Hunt eliciting as much information as he could while Quentin vacillated between being wary of Hunt and concerned about his daughter. A glance out the window confirmed that dawn was on the horizon. Not much point in trying to get back to sleep.

Hunt handed Quentin the spare disposable cell phone he'd brought with him. "This is a burner phone. Our numbers are programmed into it. You need to stay put for the time being. No trips into town. We can't take a chance on Montrose spotting you. You have to stay dead for a while longer until we can figure out what's going on. I'm firmly convinced that Roger Whitcomb's murder—"

"He was murdered?" Quentin's face paled. "The news reports never said anything about murder."

"Yes, he was murdered," Hunt continued. "I have a solid source. As I was saying, his murder and the shots fired at us are definitely connected. How and why, I don't know yet. So far, I think we've been able to keep Aurora's true identity hidden, but I doubt that will last much longer. All Montrose has to do, if he hasn't already, is pull a copy of your daughter's California driver's license, and he'll see a picture of the woman he's been face-to-face with twice and who claimed to be Gwen York."

Quentin frowned. "I can't imagine the tenacious Lt. Montrose letting that slip. He probably did it right after my car went over the cliff, if not before." He turned to face Aurora. "That's another reason I didn't try to contact you. If he even as much as suspected I was still alive…well, I didn't want him using you to track me. Or worse yet, harassing you because he thought you knew where I was hiding. Or trying to arrest you, claiming you are this mysterious accomplice."

The same possibility—more likely a probability— had occurred to Hunt, but he had kept quiet about it because he didn't want to upset Aurora. However, she was smart and resourceful. Surely, the same thought had crossed her mind.

After again making sure Quentin understood the need to stay at the cabin and securing a promise from him to do just that, Hunt and Aurora left at dawn to put their previously worked out plan into play. They met Johnny at Pirate's Cove, reversing the process they had used when they left Hunt's house the previous day. Hunt and Aurora returned to the Yacht Club in his cruiser, and Johnny picked them up in Hunt's SUV. They then drove directly to Prestige Caterers, constantly checking to make sure they weren't followed. Johnny waited in the parking lot while Hunt and Aurora went inside.

"We're talking in the area of about a hundred

people, Stu. I don't have the guest list finalized yet." Hunt carried out their plan to keep Stu busy with a non-existent party while Aurora lifted his wallet. "I don't want a sit-down dinner. I'm leaning toward something more casual. What I don't want is a tropical resort theme. That's been overused and has become way too commonplace—and boring."

Stu Allen nodded as he made notes. "Got it. No tiki torches, no grass hut bar. Is there any specific theme you *do* have in mind? Are you having us work in conjunction with a party planner," a teasing grin tugged at the corners of his mouth, "or are you dumping everything in our lap? If so, then we should have Charlie involved with this since it's more than just the menu."

Aurora poured herself a cup of coffee and one for Hunt. After handing the cup to Hunt, she bumped against Stu, spilling some coffee on herself.

"Damn! That coffee's hot." She grabbed a towel from the counter and wiped her arm. "I'm sorry, Stu. Did I spill on you, too?"

He laughed as he took another towel and wiped the counter. "No problem. Somehow, you managed to miss me."

She dabbed at the coffee stain on her shirt. "I'd better see if I can get this out before it becomes permanent." She headed for the bathroom with Stu's wallet tucked safely in the waistband of her jeans.

Stu watched her retreating form, then turned back to Hunt. "Charlie told me you had an eye for Gwen. And there's certainly some great stuff there to watch."

"Now, Stu, don't go making more of it than it is. We just went sailing, that's all. I mentioned that I had several social and business obligations to repay and thought one big party might be the best way to handle it. So…here I am. What new dishes have you been experimenting with that you could debut at my party?"

"Ah…you want to be the first of the social set to serve my new creations. Well, it just so happens that I've been toying with an entire new menu. Exactly what you're talking about. Not a sit-down dinner, but more than just hors d'oeuvres. It's sort of a multi-themed presentation—" He chuckled. "—minus the tiki torches, of course."

"Sounds promising. Tell me about it."

Hunt sat back and listened as Stu enthusiastically launched into his ideas for the menu and presentation. "I'm telling you, Hunt, this party will be the talk of the social circuit for years to come."

Aurora returned to the catering kitchen, quietly walking up behind Stu. She leaned over his shoulder, brushing against him as she looked at the preliminary menu he had drawn up. "I think you've outdone yourself, Stu. That looks fabulous." She laughed as she walked around the end of the counter. "You could even say it looks good enough to eat."

The expression on Stu's face said he appreciated the feel of her body against his. "Have you set a date for your party, Hunt?"

"Not yet." Hunt stood up. "I'm still in the early preliminary stages. I wanted to check with you on a menu and serving suggestions so I could decide on a party theme before I got any more involved in making arrangements. I'll let you know when I've made a decision and whether I'll be using an outside party planner."

"Don't wait too long. We need to get it on the

schedule as soon as possible."

The two men shook hands with Hunt promising to call, then he and Aurora left. Johnny sat in the back seat of the SUV, and Hunt slid behind the wheel with Aurora in the passenger seat. Hunt resisted the temptation to noticeably survey the surroundings. He made eye contact with Johnny in the rearview mirror. "See anything unusual while we were inside?"

"Nope. Nothing out of the ordinary. If Montrose is keeping you under surveillance, he's sure not being obvious about it. I didn't see anything that even resembled an unmarked police car, let alone a patrol car. No suspicious pedestrians hanging around on the corner or workmen who weren't really working."

They returned to Hunt's house where they gathered in the kitchen to examine what Aurora found in Stu's wallet. But first, Hunt made a call.

"Got any updated information for me, Rita?"

"What kind of information did you have in mind?" She teased, purposely stringing him along.

"Oh, you know…the usual stuff. Which of his many ugly neckties is Montrose wearing today? Did the detectives ever get their squad room painted? The latest gossip around the water cooler. Has the coroner come up with a time of death for Roger Whitcomb yet. Just the usual kind of stuff."

"Unfortunately, I only have information on one of those topics."

"I hope you aren't going to tell me about Montrose's necktie."

"Sorry…I'm afraid the only thing I have for you is a time of death on Roger."

Hunt made a mental note of the information, then

disconnected from the call. He turned toward Aurora and Johnny. "Very interesting timing. It seems Roger was killed approximately an hour before someone shot up the front of my house. More than enough time for someone to drive from Discovery Park to Medina."

"That means he was already dead when I saw someone sitting in his car."

"Dead and the killer already gone." Hunt glanced at Aurora. "What did you get from your look through Stu's wallet?"

She pulled out her burner and flipped through the images. "Stu has four credit cards. We can track his charges. There's a picture of his mother, who Johnny confirmed is real and living in Arizona just as he said. Membership cards in various organizations, most of them having to do with the culinary arts. Insurance cards for automobile insurance and health insurance. A driver's license. That was the routine stuff. In addition to that, he had a slip of paper with initials and numbers."

Hunt glanced at the pictures on her phone. "Letters and numbers with no indication of what they mean. Ten digits. No spaces and no dashes, but they look like phone numbers—both local and long distance. And the letters could be initials identifying the owner of the number."

Hunt couldn't explain it, but he instantly recognized the feeling that raced through his body and the euphoria it produced—success, achievement, everything coming together. It was the same feeling that always accompanied the moment when he was able to put the final pieces to a plan, when he knew some rare and expensive piece of jewelry was all but in his hands. He continued to stare at the numbers and letters on the paper as the exhilaration welled inside him.

"Look at these initials. DMP and DMH. How about Dan Montrose Personal and Dan Montrose Home?"

"But what would Stu be doing with phone numbers for Dan Montrose in his wallet?"

He put his arm around Aurora's waist and pulled her closer. "So he could get in touch with the lieutenant without anyone else knowing it. Montrose's personal cell phone rather than his department issued one. Perhaps an unlisted phone number at his house."

"You mean like a confidential informant?"

"Something like that." Hunt released her to pull out his phone and turned to Johnny as he forwarded the image of the numbers. "See if you can check these out, confirm who they belong to, and get a copy of the call logs if possible. While you're doing that, I'm going to check on a couple of things, then I think we can put a plan of action together that will wrap this up."

"What about my father?" Aurora's voice carried the anxiety she felt.

"He'll be with us. We can use his help. If all goes well, we should have this entire mess cleaned up in a couple of days. In fact, have him drive into town now. Tell him to call when he's a couple of blocks from my house so we can let him in through the gardener's entrance on the side. All we need to do is make sure we stay out of the way of any search warrants Montrose might come up with. Even though he doesn't have probable cause to secure one for my house and grounds, that doesn't mean he won't *create* the probable cause. I'll have my attorney be on the lookout for anything filed with the court since a search warrant needs a judge's signature."

Johnny went to the computer in Hunt's office to

check the information from Stu's wallet, first to confirm what Aurora found were actually phone numbers. It only took a few minutes to verify that one of the numbers was an unlisted phone in Montrose's house and the other one was the lieutenant's personal cell phone, just as Hunt had surmised. Johnny locked into the GPS chip in the latter so they could track Montrose in real time.

Aurora placed a call to her father, relaying Hunt's instructions.

And Hunt made a call of his own. "I need for you to arrange a location and a special setup. It has to be ready by ten o'clock tomorrow night. I can't take a chance on someone spotting Johnny, recognizing him, and associating him with me. I need discreet, quick, and no one at the location being aware of what you're doing."

****

Hunt, Aurora, Johnny, and Quentin were just finishing breakfast at the kitchen island when the phone rang. Hunt grabbed it, listened for a couple of minutes, then hung up. He turned toward three anxious faces. "The boys are ahead of schedule. Everything will be functional by five o'clock this afternoon. And that's when we'll make the call. If this produces what it's supposed to, it's a sure bet, when this is over, Lt. Montrose won't be hassling anyone ever again."

Quentin was the first to raise a concern. "Are you sure this ridiculous plan of yours is going to work? What about the people who are setting this up? Do you trust them?"

Hunt released a sigh of exasperation. "We've been over this several times. Yes, I trust the people making the arrangements. I have a long-standing relationship with them. If I didn't trust them, I wouldn't be working with them. Johnny has confirmed the phone numbers, and we've already nailed down what's going on. What we don't have is the kind of proof that can stand up in court. This will give us that proof. I've backed up everything we're doing with my attorney. He's taking care of arrangements on his end."

As with Johnny, Hunt had a long-time association with Frank Tanner. His attorney was the third person to know about his background as a cat burglar and jewel thief.

Hunt continued with his instructions. "Stu Allen is being *detained* for the time being. There's nothing left to do today except wait for five o'clock to arrive. Quentin and Aurora, you need to stay inside the house and out of sight in case we're under surveillance. Between the pool table and card table in the game room, all the movies in the media room, television, and the books in the library, you should be able to find something to do to occupy your time. I suggest everyone make sure you're well-rested since it's going to be a very long night. Perhaps a nap this afternoon."

Hunt and Johnny each took a full mug of hot coffee and walked down to the dock, out of earshot from the house. They sat and drank their coffee, something they did two or three times a month, something that wouldn't draw any suspicions from neighbors or people out on the lake. It also provided proof to anyone watching that they were both home.

Even though things appeared normal, that was far from the reality.

"I gotta tell ya, Hunt. Quentin worries me. He's too jumpy. I don't see him being able to pull this off."

"He's got me worried, too. His nerves are raw. He's

been playing dead for three months now, constantly looking over his shoulder while watching out for his daughter as best he can without letting her know he was there. I understand the stress he's been under and that he logically doesn't trust anyone at this point, including me. Or maybe that should be *especially* me. I think we need to make a couple of adjustments to our plan. We can't leave any room for error. If bullets start flying, it'll be too late to make *adjustments*."

Hunt stared at the water. A single thought continued to nag at him. "We're missing something, Johnny. Something I saw…something I heard. I'm not sure what. There's another piece to this. I think we have a solid picture of what's been happening. Stu Allen cases the heists and lets Montrose know the setup. Montrose steals the jewelry, leaves evidence pointing in whatever direction he wants, then appears on the scene the next morning as the lead detective on the case. To anyone observing his investigation, he's following all the evidence and tracking down all the leads.

"And it's been working flawlessly for five years now. He was able to make Quentin the scapegoat, but his framed suspect was able to foil him by staging his own death. We've covered everything connected to the thefts—except whatever's nagging at me."

He shook his head, frustration rampaging through him as he tried to pinpoint what was wrong, what he was missing.

"That only covers our scenario of how the jewelry thefts happen. It doesn't connect someone shooting at you or Roger's murder—if that's part of this." Johnny leveled a serious look at Hunt. "And I believe it's connected."

Hunt returned his concern. "So do I. Murder and attempted murder is not part of my arrangement with Leo Jordan, but it would be nice to wrap that up along with the jewelry."

They talked for a while longer, fine-tuning their plan while drinking their coffee. Finally, Johnny rose from his chair. "I'm going to check the security recordings from overnight to see if there's anyone watching the house."

Johnny headed toward the guest house while Hunt took their coffee cups to the kitchen. Aurora met him at the door.

"What was all that about?" She gestured toward the dock. "Is something wrong?"

He ran his fingertips lightly across her cheek. "No, nothing's wrong. We do that a couple of times a month—brainstorming investigative techniques, discussing the current case, exchanging information about new gadgets on the market. We didn't want to break the routine, in case someone's watching."

And the thought continued to pick at his consciousness. He had missed something. He went back over everything in his mind, but nothing jumped out at him. The rest of the day passed slowly. He saw the same tension on everyone else that continued to assault his senses. If only he could put his finger on that loose puzzle piece that kept circling around him while refusing to land. A tightness pulled across his chest. He drew in a deep breath in an attempt to break the uncomfortable feeling but to no avail.

Finally, the hour came—five o'clock. He turned his attention to Johnny. "Let's do it."

The laptop computer dialed the number of the Seattle police department using one of the disposable phones. Johnny typed in the text and the computer-generated voice said the words. "Lt. Montrose." When the lieutenant came on the line, Johnny typed in the message for the computer to say. "If you want to find the very much alive Quentin Brentano, be at the old Alaska Hotel by Pioneer Square. He'll be in room twenty-seven at eight o'clock in the morning. He's been staying there the last month and will be back tomorrow to meet with someone."

"Where is he now? Who is this?"

The only response was a click as Johnny disconnected the call.

Chapter Nine

"This is from five hours ago." Johnny played back the video recording as Hunt, Aurora, and Quentin watched. The camera in the motor home parked across the street from the Alaska Hotel had picked up Lt. Montrose going into the building. The time code in the upper corner of the recording registered one o'clock that morning. Then the camera hidden in room twenty-seven clearly showed the lieutenant entering the second-floor room moments later.

They continued to watch the recording from their position in the motor home as Montrose looked around, checked dresser drawers and the closet for clothes, then shuffled through some papers on the bed. The camera had a clear view of the smile on his face when he found Quentin's name on an envelope.

"Here's the best part." Johnny sounded pleased with the results of his all-night surveillance. "He's wearing latex gloves to avoid leaving fingerprints, but that won't mean a thing when this recording is produced as evidence."

Montrose removed several pieces of jewelry from his pocket, placed them in a cloth bag, and hid them under the mattress. After checking to make sure everything in the room was exactly as he found it, the lieutenant quickly left and was immediately picked up on the other camera as he departed the hotel.

"That's perfect, Johnny. Absolutely no doubt about what he's doing or his identity." The ringing of Hunt's disposable cell intruded. He answered it, listened for a minute, then disconnected from the call. "Montrose got his search warrant ten minutes ago. It's a *no-knock* warrant, which means he can break the door down and enter without warning. Nothing to do now but get everyone into position and wait."

But waiting was easier said than done. Anxiety churned in the pit of Hunt's stomach. After all these years, he was about to catch Lt. Montrose in a sting operation. All these years of *knowing* Montrose was more than simply over-zealous in his duties but not being able to pursue the truth for fear of exposing his own illegal activities. But with the statute of limitations having rendered an arrest for Hunt's last burglary no longer legal—no new arrests made—he welcomed the opportunity to nail the arrogant and despicable Lt. Montrose to the wall.

Within fifteen minutes, everyone involved had assembled in the RV. They did a last-minute confirmation of the plan and everyone's function. The original plan called for Quentin to be in the hotel room when Montrose arrived, especially since that was who the lieutenant expected to see. But Hunt changed the plan so that it would be Aurora and Hunt himself who would be there instead. It was more than concern about Quentin being able to pull it off in his rattled state of mind with his nerves raw. Hunt needed her steady hand for a critical move but only if she agreed. She assured Hunt she could handle it in spite of the danger.

Tension etched her face. He wanted to pull her into his arms and comfort her, but it was neither the time nor the place. Instead, he reached out for her hand, wanting some sort of physical contact.

"This is the part that plays havoc with the nerves. It will all be over very soon. All Montrose has to do is show up, search the room, find the pieces of stolen jewelry, and attempt to arrest us for possession of stolen property. Then we'll have him. Even if for some obscure reason this doesn't stick in court, he'll lose his badge and be subject to civil action. Quentin will be cleared of any wrongdoing and can return to his normal routine."

Aurora slowly shook her head as if trying to sort it all out in her mind. "It sounds so simple and straight forward the way you say it. I hope I don't mess up my part."

He gave her hand a confident squeeze. "You'll be fine. Just keep yourself focused on the goal and be prepared for the unexpected."

She returned the squeeze. "I hope that *unexpected* doesn't prove to be a disaster for us. There's no way Montrose will be here alone. He's implementing a search warrant, which means he'll have other officers with him."

"Yes. That's the part we'll have to wing—the unknown factor. But nothing can negate the fact that we have a timed and dated recording showing Montrose hiding pieces of stolen jewelry at a specific location several hours before he requested a search warrant for that same location, a search warrant based on what he conveniently claimed was an *anonymous* tip."

A string of phone calls kept them apprised of Montrose's movements and location, the last call saying he was leaving the station and would be at the hotel in approximately ten minutes—Montrose alone in his unmarked car and two uniformed officers in a patrol car. Only two officers rather than a SWAT team. A no-knock warrant was usually accompanied by more force than two uniformed officers.

Hunt looked at Aurora. "That's our cue. Let's go."

Quentin's anxiety was written all over his face. "Be careful, Rora."

"Don't worry, daddy, I will."

Hunt and Aurora dashed across the street and up the stairs to room twenty-seven where Hunt positioned himself by the window so he could see when Montrose arrived. No matter how hard he tried, Hunt couldn't shake the notion that he had missed something important. Something right at his fingertips, yet just out of reach.

A straightforward investigation to locate stolen property for the insurance company had exploded into a true puzzle with many levels, including the murder of a police detective. They had soundly nailed down the solution to the original problem…the string of jewelry thefts. They now knew the who, so the location of the missing property would be forthcoming. And in the process, Aurora had achieved her goal of proving her father's innocence along with the happy added fact of discovering he was alive. That would finalize his investigation for Excellence Insurance, but it left way too many loose ends unresolved. And the biggest loose end was who shot at them and why.

And whether it was connected to Roger Whitcomb's murder.

"Ballistics! How could I have forgotten?" He stared at her as he berated himself for the oversight.

She looked at him quizzically. "What about

ballistics?"

"A comparison of the bullets fired at us and the one that killed Whitcomb. If they came from the same weapon that would definitely tie the two shootings together."

"Can you call—"

"No, not for this." He had to stop her before she mentioned Rita's name. No good could come from revealing his inside source in the Seattle police department to the people in the RV parked across the street who were watching and listening. "Discovery Park in Seattle and my house in Medina are two separate law enforcement jurisdictions, thus two separate incidents resulting in two separate investigations with no outwardly obvious connection."

He knitted his brow into a scowl. "Damn. That's no good. Whitcomb was shot at close range with a small caliber weapon. Whoever shot at us did it from a distance…all the way down my driveway and across the street to the neighbor's trash barrels. A small caliber weapon wouldn't be viable for that. Apparently, I just shot down my own theory."

He spotted the police cars pulling up in front of the hotel. An immediate adrenaline surge hit him. "They're here. Are you ready?"

Aurora flashed a somewhat tentative smile. "I'm as ready as I'll ever be."

He looked directly at the hidden camera, addressing his comments to the people in the motorhome. "It's show time!"

They quickly moved to their predetermined positions, Hunt sitting on the bed reading the morning newspaper and Aurora walking out the bathroom door.

Then they waited for Montrose to *discover* them.

The door from the hallway swung open with a loud crash when one of the officers kicked it in. The three men rushed into the room with guns drawn. Hunt and Aurora both feigned surprise at the break-in as Hunt jumped to his feet and took a step toward the door before coming to a halt.

Montrose's expression flashed from shock, to surprise, and finally delight. He walked over to Hunt, his service weapon still in his hand. A broad smile spread across his face, showing the arrogance of a man who thought he had hit the jackpot.

"This is better than I'd hoped. I came looking for Quentin Brentano, and instead, I find his daughter—" He shot Aurora a smug look of superiority that said she hadn't fooled him for a minute. "—and Huntington Wolfe III. Not a prayer you're going to be able to wrangle your way out of it this time, Hunt. Your fancy lawyer won't be able to help you. I caught you red-handed with the goods."

"What goods? The only thing you caught me with is the morning newspaper and a woman of legal age who's here of her own free will. We're not in a compromising position and are both fully clothed." He gestured toward the policemen who had accompanied Montrose. "As these two fine officers will be able to testify."

A flicker of hesitation crossed the lieutenant's face, but he quickly recovered. "A woman who has been hiding behind a false identity, which she used when giving a police report about that alleged shooting at your house."

"I believe that's the Medina police, not your jurisdiction. And the wound on my arm along with the bullets the police dug out from the door frame of my house says the shooting wasn't *alleged*. It was real."

"I'm head of the task force investigating the jewelry thefts, so anything connected—"

"You're saying the shooting at my house had something to do with all those robberies?" He scowled at Montrose. "How did you come to that astonishing determination?"

Montrose glared at him for a moment. Hunt could almost see the wheels turning in his head trying to figure out how to handle the blunder without making the officers in the room suspicious. He barked out orders to the two officers. "Search this room. Turn it inside out and upside down if you have to."

But it wasn't Montrose's only blunder. The other one was far more glaring and telling of the lieutenant's intentions. He hadn't searched either one of them, not for contraband and especially not for weapons. The stage had been set.

Montrose returned his attention to Hunt, paused, then took two menacing steps forward as he visibly tightened his hold on his gun.

It was the opening Aurora had been waiting for. She caught the look Hunt threw her way then moved quickly to handle her crucial part of the plan. "Don't hurt him!" She literally threw herself between Montrose and Hunt, bumping the lieutenant in the process. "It's not his fault. I'm the one—"

"Shut up!" Hunt's voice contained just the proper combination of anger and frustration as he grabbed her arm and yanked her away from Montrose. Even though Hunt had handled her roughly, as she anticipated, she still found the physical contact reassuring. He had managed to impart a confidence and sense that everything would be okay. He looked so in control and calm, a far cry from the anxiety churning in the pit of her stomach. In spite of that, she could not deny the tingle of excitement coursing through her.

The sensation of the magazine from Montrose's gun tucked safely in the waist of her jeans helped to soothe her nerves. It had been a risky move, one that Hunt said he didn't want her to try unless she was positive she could handle it. But it went smoothly. Montrose didn't show any indication that he knew she had removed the magazine from his gun while the weapon was in his hand. It was the one move Hunt had been concerned about. After seeing how nervous Quentin was about the plan, he wanted Quentin to stay in the RV with everyone else.

Montrose waved his gun at them. "Both of you, stand over there by the wall and don't move."

Montrose held back, allowing the other officers to eventually find the hidden jewelry so it would appear he had never handled it. No one would be able to accuse him of any impropriety. She had to fight to keep the grin from tugging at the corners of her mouth. That smug look wouldn't be on his face much longer. And knowing that helped settle the nervous tension that continued to assault her senses and churn in the pit of her stomach.

She glanced at Hunt. The set of his jaw, the look in his eyes, the way he moved his fingers… She knew him well enough by now to recognize the signs that something serious was going through his mind. Something much more than a simple review of their plan. He had not looked directly at the hidden camera, the signal to people in the RV to implement the rest of the plan. He suddenly looked up, glanced at her, then stared at Montrose as if mentally boring a hole through the lieutenant's head. Whatever Hunt had been pondering, he had come to a definite conclusion.

"We've got something, lieutenant." The excited shout came from the officer who pulled up the mattress while the other officer grabbed the cloth pouch from where Montrose had put it. He emptied the contents onto a table.

"Good work, men." Montrose reached into his jacket pocket and withdrew a piece of paper. "Here, see if any of those pieces match this list of stolen items."

The two officers sorted through the jewelry with gloved hands, checking each piece of jewelry against the list. "Every one of these matches a description of a stolen item."

"Put it all back in the pouch and give it to me." The officers did as they were instructed.

Hunt spoke up. "We've never seen that before. It was obviously left by a previous occupant of this room." His voice was controlled, revealing nothing of what he was feeling or thinking. Try as she might, Aurora could not read what was going on in his mind.

Montrose wasn't able to control the sneer that curled his lip. "Yeah, a previous occupant by the name of Quentin Brentano. The man you're here to meet. Brentano stole it, then took himself out of the picture and let his daughter carry on. But you, Hunt, I thought you were smarter than this. I guess this is what happens when you believe your own reputation and hype, consider yourself untouchable. You rich boys are all the same. You think your family name and money mean the rules don't apply to you. I guess you're about to find out that's not true."

Montrose turned his attention to the two officers. "I need both of you downstairs. One of you move the patrol car out of sight, and the other one roust the manager of this dump out of bed and get his records. I want the signature and a description of the person who checked into this room. I'll bet they both point squarely at Quentin Brentano. Then wait downstairs for him to show up. He should be here in about fifteen minutes. My source said eight o'clock."

"But lieutenant…that will leave you here alone with—"

"Don't worry about me. The only thing Wolfe here knows how to do is hide behind his high-priced fancy lawyer. Now, get that car moved before Brentano sees it."

Again, Aurora marveled at Hunt's calm demeanor. Montrose's obvious attempts to bait him weren't working. He didn't even get a small rise out of Hunt, let alone a reaction. But the entire mood of the room changed as soon as the officers left.

Hunt moved away from the wall and to the side. She immediately recognized him putting some distance between himself and her knowing that Montrose could not effectively deal with both positions at the same time. Montrose was twenty years older than Hunt, a couple of inches shorter, and about thirty pounds overweight…not a physical threat. And she had the bullets from Montrose's gun. So, what was Hunt concerned about?

"What now, lieutenant?" Hunt took another step farther away from her. "You've given yourself a ten-minute window here. You know as well as I do that this frame will never stick. As you mentioned, I have an excellent attorney. You have no proof that either one of us"—he indicated Aurora—"had any knowledge of what was hidden under that mattress. You're certainly not going to find any of our fingerprints on the jewelry. I also noticed that they were minor pieces with the important ones still missing. For instance, I didn't see the Swanson's emerald pendant. Do you have a ready explanation for that?"

"I don't need to explain it. I have the two of you and stolen jewelry in the same room and a valid search warrant. I don't need anything else."

"You'll definitely need an explanation for why you found it necessary to send away any witnesses, then gunned down two unarmed people."

Aurora's breath froze in her lungs. A hard jolt of adrenaline raced through her veins. Had she heard him correctly? Lt. Montrose planned to kill them? He still had the gun, but she had the bullets. Hunt knew that. Was he just baiting Montrose? Trying to get him to incriminate himself on the recording even more than he already had? When Hunt said they'd have to wing it, this wasn't what she had anticipated.

"Unarmed? Well, I'll probably have to suffer a departmental reprimand for failing to search you. And since I haven't actually arrested you, I didn't have cause to handcuff you. Yes, I'll need to admit to a momentary lapse in following proper procedures. But I think it will be overlooked when it's discovered that the gun you had is the same one that killed detective Whitcomb."

"You're the one who killed Roger?" She blurted out the words before she could stop them. "But why would you kill your own partner?"

She glanced at Hunt and saw him look directly at the

hidden camera and give a subtle nod of his head. That eased her panic a bit. Then she saw Montrose withdraw a small caliber handgun from an ankle holster. That one had bullets. Her renewed panic combined with a growing fear. It would take possibly as much as a full minute for help to reach them from the RV. Their carefully constructed plan was falling apart right in front of her.

"Simple answer, Aurora. He must have overheard Roger calling me. Apparently, his partner on the police force was not his partner in crime. Roger didn't know who to trust, but he did know the lieutenant and I were bitter adversaries. Roger wanted to align himself with me and use my attorney to protect himself. Montrose's partner in crime was a position held by Stu Allen."

A look of surprise darted across Montrose's face at the mention of Stu's name.

Hunt took a moment's delight in Montrose's reaction. "Oh…did I forget to mention that Stu Allen is in custody? My guess is that the DA's office is cutting a deal with him at this moment."

The lieutenant quickly recovered his composure. "That's not going to work, Hunt. You're not going to bluff me into believing you actually know anything. Now, a shot in the wall behind me with the weapon that will be found on you and two shots from my service weapon in self-defense."

"You arrogant bastard. You really think you're going to get away with—"

A shot rang out as Montrose quickly fired a shot over his shoulder to put the bullet into the wall behind him fired from the murder weapon that killed Roger. Then he leveled his service weapon at Hunt. Aurora froze to the spot, her eyes wide in fear. It had all happened so suddenly.

Just as Montrose squeezed off the shot, Hunt lunged toward Aurora to shove her into the bathroom and out of the line of fire. At that moment, the door burst open with a loud crash. The sound and activity startled the lieutenant just as he pulled the trigger. The shot from his official service weapon went wild.

Hunt immediately charged toward Montrose, knocking him to the floor. He landed a solid punch to the lieutenant's jaw before Johnny intervened and pulled him back. Two of the officers who had been in the RV monitoring the entire operation took charge of Montrose. They searched him for additional weapons, then put him in handcuffs.

Hunt helped Aurora up from the floor, then raised a questioning eyebrow as he looked at her. She pulled the magazine from the waist of her jeans and held it up, showing him that she had taken it from Montrose's gun as planned. Her expression conveyed the same confusion that ran through him. "Then where the hell did that bullet come from?"

Quentin rushed into the room followed by Frank Tanner. He went straight to his daughter and hugged her. "Are you okay, Rora?"

"I'll be fine, daddy, as soon as I get my heart started again."

Quentin glanced over his shoulder at Hunt. "I guess you forgot about the round in the chamber."

Hunt nodded with a sheepish grin. "Yeah, I think you're right."

"Nicely done, Hunt." His attorney's voice grabbed his attention. Frank Tanner's part of the operation had been to arrange for an assistant DA and police officers to be present in the RV. For that, Frank had turned to his golfing buddy, the chief of police. "Was that stuff you said about detective Whitcomb wanting to go through you to engage my services true?"

"I have no idea, Frank. I was playing it by ear. It was the only thing that made any sense to me. Even with Stu Allen's confession about the jewel thefts, we were still flying blind as far as solid facts were concerned. Especially since Stu didn't have any connection to Whitcomb's murder."

"How did you know it was Montrose who killed him?"

"I suspected but didn't know for sure until a few minutes ago. Something had been nagging at me...something I saw or heard but couldn't remember. Then it hit me. It was something Quentin said while we were at the cabin that finally brought all the pieces together."

"Something I said?" Quentin turned his attention to Hunt and Frank. "What could I have said? I didn't know anything. My only concern was to keep a watchful eye on Aurora."

"Remember when I asked you if you had been watching my house the night someone took a shot at us? You became quite upset when you learned Aurora could have been shot. You said you drove by, saw Montrose, and left so he wouldn't spot you, yet you weren't aware of the shooting."

"Yes, that's what happened. I didn't see anything."

"You saw the missing piece to the puzzle. You didn't know about someone taking a shot at us. That means, when you drove by my house, the police weren't swarming around in front, no crime scene tape, nothing to indicate that anything had happened, not even a 911 call to report a shooting. Yet you saw Montrose at my house before anything happened even though he claimed to have heard about the shooting and showed up after the Medina police were on the scene. He claimed to have arrived at the same time as the crime scene technicians. The only way you could have seen Montrose in front of my house was if he had been there before the shots were fired. He shot Roger, then drove straight to my house."

"Mr. Brentano," the assistant DA addressed Quentin as he approached him, "I'll need a statement from you concerning…well, I guess about everything from when you were first questioned by Lt. Montrose, you faking your own death, and ending up here this morning. And Mr. Wolfe," he turned toward Hunt, "I'll need a statement from you, too."

"I'll stop by your office tomorrow morning if that's convenient."

"Yes. Maybe around ten o'clock?"

"Will you also need Aurora?"

"Yes, if you could both come to my office."

The assistant DA left with Quentin. The officers read Montrose his rights and took him away. Hunt's attorney started to leave, but Hunt stopped him.

"Frank…one moment, please."

"Is something wrong?"

"No, it's just that, in spite of all this, the only jewelry that's been recovered are a few minor pieces that Montrose planted here. I still need to recover several high-dollar items to fulfill my contract with Excellence Insurance. See what you can do about procuring access to whatever Montrose might have in the way of a safe deposit box at a bank or maybe a safe at his house. The merchandise has never shown up anywhere so he must still have it."

Frank chuckled as he shook his head in amusement. "I'll see what I can do. You identified the thief and his accomplice and topped that off by catching the murderer of a police officer. I'm sure the DA can be persuaded to give you credit for the recovery of the jewels."

Hunt took a calming breath, then grasped Aurora's hand and led her outside. "Alone at last." He pulled her into his embrace. "Now that everything is behind us, I want to give you my full attention...for as long as you want it."

She brushed a soft kiss across his lips. "I think it's safe to say that will be for quite a while, if that's okay with you."

"It's more than okay."

Epilogue

Hunt rolled over onto his back, taking Aurora with him so that her body rested on top of his. He ran his hand down her bare bottom, reveling in the creamy texture of her skin. "I suppose, Ms. Brentano, we should think about getting out of bed, unless you'd like to spend the entire day here." He nibbled seductively at her earlobe. "Something that would be quite okay with me."

"That's a very tempting offer, Mr. Wolfe. But you know we're due at the assistant DA's office at ten o'clock. That's in two hours."

"You're right. We should probably hit the shower."

She laughed. "*We* probably shouldn't. You know what happened last time we showered together."

"I remember every exciting moment of it." He placed a tender kiss on her lips, then reluctantly let go of her.

Aurora slipped out of bed and disappeared into the bathroom. Hunt pulled on a pair of sweatpants and went downstairs to make some coffee. He spotted the large priority mail envelope on the kitchen island. *Hmm….Johnny must have put this here.* He looked at the return address. No name, just a post office box. It was postmarked four days ago. Priority Mail sent locally should have arrived the next day.

A hint of apprehension worked its way into his reality. He stared at the envelope, not sure what to do. He hit the intercom button and buzzed Johnny in the guest house. "Where did this envelope come from?"

"The carrier delivered it about fifteen minutes ago. I had to sign for it. He apologized for the delay. It should have been delivered two days ago."

"You had to sign for it? That means someone had to do more than just hand it to a clerk at the post office. There isn't any name as part of the return, just a post office box."

"I didn't notice anything hard in it. It feels like it's only paper."

Hunt continued to stare at the envelope, uncertain about how to handle it. It was the timing as it related to Roger's murder that had him on edge. Montrose knew Roger had called him. Could Montrose have suspected what Roger might do? Had Montrose sent the envelope? Had he sent something lethal? Perhaps a letter bomb?

"What's this?" Aurora slipped her arm around his waist as she indicated the envelope.

"I'm not sure." He brought her up to date on how it happened to be on the counter.

"Do you think we should call the bomb squad?"

"I don't know. It feels like paper, nothing hard or stiff. But that doesn't rule out something explosive or even the possibility of something powdery that would scatter and be inhaled when the envelope was opened, such as fentanyl."

"If you're not concerned about it exploding, can you open it at a distance?"

He buzzed Johnny again. "Did you run this through your X-ray gizmo to check what's inside it?"

"Yes. Nothing suspicious showed up."

"Okay, thanks."

Hunt impulsively reached for Aurora, pulling her into his arms. "I thought all of this was behind us. Nothing left to do but give our statements to the DA and then testify in court. And now, here's this. It's postmarked in the afternoon and Roger called that same evening."

"Do you suppose"—a slight frown marred her brow—"that this is from Roger? He mailed this to you, then called?"

"We're about to find out." He took it into his office and used the paper cutter to snip off the bottom edge rather than opening it by pulling the designated tab at the top. He carefully removed the contents, stared at the papers, then allowed an audible sigh of relief.

"It's okay. It's from Roger Whitcomb." He picked up the papers and did a quick perusal. "Interesting. This seems to be all the backup information Roger had, stuff he'd been collecting for a while. Probably what he wanted to talk to us about. It seems Roger had been suspicious of Montrose for quite a while but didn't know who to take it to—who might believe him over Montrose. It looks like we have something to take with us when we see the assistant DA this morning. This should be a great help in the case against Montrose."

"Won't the fact that you opened the envelope compromise the evidence?"

"The post office has Johnny's signature showing what time it was delivered this morning."

Aurora gave him a meaningful look. "And speaking of this morning, we need to get ready."

"Let me make a copy of all this before I turn it over to the DA."

When he finished making the copies, Hunt took

Aurora's hand. He voiced a thought that had been running through his mind, one he had been struggling with for a while. "I have an idea. After we finish with our statements this morning, let's go away somewhere. Anywhere you want. We can take the cabin cruiser and go either up or down the coast. Or we can hop in the jet and head for Europe. Wherever you say."

"I don't know, Hunt. I have an apartment in San Francisco that's been sitting vacant for three months. I have a job I need to get back to. I can't expect my boss to hold it for me indefinitely. This entire experience has been a roller coaster ride...anticipation, panic, thrills, fear, then it starts all over again. Everything I've done and thought has been controlled by outside forces. I mean...do we really know each other at all?"

As much as she wanted to go with him, to throw caution to the wind and follow her heart, she didn't want to end up in a situation where he felt trapped because she wasn't who he thought she was, one where the emotional turmoil they had shared had created a false sense of emotional bonding. They hadn't discussed anything about a relationship. She hadn't dared to think it, to allow the word *love* to enter her thoughts. And in reality, they had known each other for a very short period of time, especially compared to *forever*.

"What we said yesterday about spending a long time getting to know each other... I meant every word of it. Don't go. Give up your apartment. Quit your job." He had managed to get that much out. He knew he was venturing into unknown territory. Affairs? He'd had numerous, some of them somewhat serious. But he had never met *the* woman, the one who would win his heart. Not until now. He placed a loving kiss on her lips. "Stay with me."

"Are you sure?"

"I've never been so sure of anything in my life. But if it makes you more comfortable, we'll give it a test period...a specific amount of time."

Confusion clouded her mind. Was he offering a commitment or just a short-term affair? "What kind of a time frame are you thinking?"

"How does fifty years sound to you? If that works out, then we can extend it."

A huge wave of relief swept through her. It was all she needed to hear. She wrapped her arms around his neck. "It sounds like a reasonable test."

"Good. Let's get dressed and go to the DA's office to take care of our business. Then maybe we could stop by the licensing bureau and check out marriage licenses...just out of curiosity."

Joy, like she'd never known before, flooded her heart. It had all been so simple, so unassuming. No formal declaration. Just a lifetime commitment. "Sounds like a good plan to me..." She offered a teasing grin. "...just out of curiosity."

A word about the author…

I've lived most of my life in Los Angeles and earned my living for twenty years by working in television production. I was always interested in writing and dabbled at it, but not seriously. I combined my interest in writing with my avocation of photography and began doing magazine articles featuring my photographs. After selling several articles, I discovered I enjoyed the writing process as much as the photography.

My friends told me I should make use of my television contacts and write scripts. I enrolled in a screen writing class at UCLA. By the close of class I knew screen writing was not for me. The other thing I knew was that I wanted to write novels rather than magazine articles.

Contact Shawna at:
www.shawnadelacorte.com
https://shawnadelacorte.blogspot.com

Thank you for purchasing
this publication of The Wild Rose Press, Inc.

For questions or more information
contact us at
info@thewildrosepress.com.

The Wild Rose Press, Inc.
www.thewildrosepress.com